THE TICK™

Six Action-Packed Adventures

Stories by **Clay Griffith**

Based on characters created by Ben Edlund

A Skylark Book

Toronto New York London Sydney Auckland

RL4.6, All Ages

THE TICK—SIX ACTION-PACKED ADVENTURES
A Skylark Book / October 1994

*Skylark Books is a registered trademark of Bantam Books,
a division of Bantam Doubleday Dell Publishing Group, Inc.
Registered in U.S. Patent and Trademark Office and elsewhere.*

THE TICK—Six Action-Packed Adventures *is based on original screenplays by
Ben Edlund and Richard Liebmann-Smith.*

ISBN 0-553-48301-3

Published simultaneously in the United States and Canada

---

*Bantam Books are published by Bantam Books, a division of Bantam Doubleday
Dell Publishing Group, Inc. Its trademark, consisting of the words "Bantam
Books" and the portrayal of a rooster, is Registered in U.S. Patent and Trademark
Office and in other countries. Marca Registrada. Bantam Books, 1540 Broadway,
New York, New York 10036.*

PRINTED IN THE UNITED STATES OF AMERICA

0   9   8   7   6   5   4   3   2   1

Contents

Part 1

THE TICK
FINDS HIS
DESTINY

1

A Long Bus Trip to Destiny

"Destiny."

The Tick thought about his destiny as he rode along on the night bus to Reno, Nevada. He flicked on the overhead light above his seat. Other sleepy passengers groaned. In his big blue hands he clutched the latest issue of *Leotard Legends,* the leading superhero trade magazine.

"Destiny is a funny kick in the tights: I am destined to be a superhero," said the Tick. "It is no simple path. It's a winding, boulder-strewn path lined with a thousand easy deaths. And no dental plan. My cares—many. My pleasures—few. My legs—cramped!"

"Nnnng!" he screamed. "Leg cramp!"

"Shhh!" the other passengers hissed.

The Tick tried to relieve the leg cramps by shifting his muscular, seven-foot-tall, four-hundred-pound superhero body around in his little bus seat. The couple in the seat in front of him were squashed forward. They muttered angrily. Surrounded by his magazines and crumpled snack packages, the Tick began to think out loud again.

"I am on a pilgrimage to Reno, Nevada," the Tick continued. The crowd on the bus groaned again. "There I will be judged, and assigned a city." He spoke louder in his excitement. "My very own city to protect from the ravages of evil and Super Villainy!"

"*Shhhh!*" the other passengers warned.

"Hey!" the Tick responded. "I'm narrating here!"

As the bus continued to roll through the dark desert night, the Tick stared out the window. "This bus has become my air-conditioned prison!" He couldn't get comfortable, thrashing in his seat. "Monotony is devouring my mind!"

Suddenly, through the window of the bus, the Tick saw a sign for Motel 0. It read: WELCOME, SUPERHEROES!

"Drivesman!" the Tick shouted suddenly. "Stop the bus! I'm getting off!" And the bus left him standing in the motel parking lot with his magazines and snack wrappers.

"All the best new superheroes have come to this place," the Tick said to himself. "To compete for the best city in the country to protect." He thought hard. "How to win the nation's most challenging city? This is going to take a real spectacle!"

The Tick saw an auto repair shop across the street. An idea surged into his superbrain.

"Hey! Tools!"

Later that night, the superhero convention was in full swing inside the Motel 0. It was a festive event. The suave Barry Barrymore was master of ceremonies. He introduced the legendary heroes who would judge the youngsters. They were famous crime fighters. The first one was the peaceable Earth Quaker, who wore a suit of rocks and whose rumbling stomach could shake any criminal to his knees. Also there was Rubber Justice, the World's Stretchiest Man. The Fiery Flame had set fire to the tablecloth on the judges' table accidentally. All the fresh, young superheroes fidgeted nervously around the room while their parents straightened their capes, tightened their masks, or adjusted the liquid oxygen mix on their Insta-Flame jetpacks.

All heads turned when the Tick entered the room. He was dragging a gigantic contraption. It was a twelve-foot steel box covered with auto parts, hammers, spikes, blades, and a bucket seat from a 1977 American Motors Gremlin. The clerk at the door asked for the Tick's invitation.

The Tick said heroically, "Lists! Cards! Forms! Fear is for the fearful! Think big!" And he continued dragging his giant metal thing into the room. "Watch your feet!"

"Oww!" yelled several heroes whose toes were run over.

By the time the Tick reached the stage, cities had already been assigned. Torso Porcupine got Detroit. He was so excited, he accidentally fired several of his razor-sharp quills at the judges. And Friendly Fire, who was the son of the Fiery Flame, one of the judges, got New Rochelle.

"Excuse me!" the Tick called out as he dragged his huge metal box up to the stage. He pulled an extension cord out of it. "Anyone see an outlet? Ah-ha!" He plugged in his box, which immediately emitted a deep hum. The judges exchanged worried looks.

"Just last night I was thinking." The Tick addressed the room of assembled might. "How can I best express my superheroness? I come to you, across an ocean of adversity—and a really long bus ride! But how to prove my worth as a hero? And then it came to me: Build something! Something capable of superhuman punishment. A terrible engine of destruction. A big, harmful thing!

"Ladies and gentlemen, I am the Tick!" The Tick strapped himself into the bucket seat attached to the contraption. "I am as strong as I need to be, and nigh invulnerable." He liked to use the word *nigh*. It meant the same as *almost* or *nearly*, but it sounded way cooler.

"I demonstrate!" The Tick turned a dial on his machine. Loud, dramatic music blared out of a speaker attached to the thing. The Tick pulled a lever and held on tightly. The machine hummed louder and rumbled. Then everything went haywire. Arms sprung, wires snapped, and sparks showered. A small hammer swung down and hit the Tick on the head.

"Gaaa," he said, surprised. Then he remembered something else that his machine could do and he reached for another lever. *Boom!*

Police reports said later that the flames shooting from the roof of the Motel 0 could be seen as far away as Holtville, California.

The next day the Tick was on the bus heading out of Reno. He was happy that no one had been hurt during his demonstration. "They gave me a city!" he said softly and happily to himself. Then louder, "They gave me a *city*! Destiny's powerful hand has made the bed of my future, and it's up to me to lie in it." The Tick was overcome by emotion for a second.

6

Then he spoke again. "Out there, my city lies: unprotected, unloved, crying out for a champion to call its own." The Tick studied the giant road map that he spread over his seat and over the annoyed people sitting in front of him. He wasn't far away now. He looked at the white card that had been given to him in Reno with the name of his assignment. It read "The City."

"The City," he said in awe. "My The City. It cries to me of its need!"

2

Enter: Arthur!

"Arthur?"

Arthur swiveled his office chair to look up at his supervisor. "Yes, Mr. Wiederspahn?"

Mr. Wiederspahn struggled to say what was on his mind. "Arthur. I—I'm afraid the Firm feels that it's time to allow you the opportunity to pursue other avenues of employment."

Arthur stared at his boss. "I'm fired? But why? Is there a problem with my work?"

Mr. Wiederspahn bit his lip. "No, Arthur." He hesitated, searching for the right words, but then he just blurted out, "It's that stupid bunny outfit!"

"Oh, no, no." Arthur corrected Mr. Wiederspahn gently. "Not a bunny suit, sir—moth. It's my moth suit." Arthur looked at himself. He was wearing a skintight white costume, which was a bit of a fashion risk because Arthur was a little hefty. He wore goggles, and on his head were feathery antennae, which people often mistook for bunny ears. "Actually it's a flying suit. The wings are in my briefcase." Arthur lifted his briefcase from under his desk and shook it. There was a clattering sound from inside. He smiled.

Mr. Wiederspahn said, "Arthur, you're making the other accountants nervous. We all find this kind of rampant individuality very disturbing."

Arthur stood up. "I know you think I'm crazy, Mr. Wiederspahn, but I'm not! It's just . . ." He stared upward. "Ever since I found this suit, I've felt strange new needs . . . urges. . . . I—I can't live this life a moment longer! Somewhere out there, a destiny of adventure and excitement waits for me!" Arthur marched between the long rows of accountants, all punching their calculators. One of them looked up, momentarily inspired by the stirring scene. Mr. Wiederspahn had never seen this heroic side of Arthur.

Arthur continued, "Accounting is a fine skill to fall back on, but the road less traveled—much less traveled— the moth-suit-and-wings road, is a lot more exciting than taxes!" And Arthur walked proudly out of the office.

As Arthur wandered the streets of the City thinking about how to begin his new career as a superhero, the Tick was getting off the bus from Reno.

"City!" the Tick cried with excitement. "It is I, the Tick! Your destined defender! Show me where it hurts!" He gazed around him at the wondrous skyscrapers.

"Tall!" he exclaimed.

He went directly to the top of the tallest building and

gazed out over the City. "There's crime here," he said, adopting a heroic pose. "I can smell it."

Then the Tick started his first official patrol. He searched for crime by leaping from building to building. With each mighty leap he cried *"Hep!"* then *"Huht!"* then *"Ho!"* With each powerful bound he chipped ledges, broke stone edges off skyscrapers, and bent television aerials. He didn't mean to. But the Tick was a very strong leaper.

At one point he tried a very difficult double flip off a twenty-story building, but missed it and plummeted toward the ground. Normally a superhero saved himself from falling by grabbing a flagpole. In fact, flagpoles were put on buildings to save superheroes from falls. But the Tick was very big and when he grabbed the flagpole, it broke. He crashed to the ground right next to where Arthur was walking. Arthur looked down into the big hole that the Tick had made in the street.

The Tick let out a roar of pain. Then he looked up at Arthur. "Gravity is a harsh mistress," he said wisely.

"Are you all right?" Arthur asked.

"I'm fine." The Tick smiled. "I'm nigh invulnerable. I'm built for this kind of thing." He noticed Arthur's moth costume. "Nice outfit."

Arthur helped the Tick out of the crater. "Are you a superhero?" he asked.

"Known to evildoers everywhere as the Tick!"

"I'm Arthur. Known to taxpayers everywhere as the accountant. I'm looking for adventure."

The Tick put his arm around Arthur's shoulders. He had been in the City for only a few minutes and he already had a partner.

"Come have lunch with me, Arthur," the Tick said. "Adventure will follow."

At the nearby Silver 50s diner, the Tick and Arthur sat at the counter. At the end of the counter was a man who looked unhappy. A second man sat two stools down from the Tick. He was dressed like a mild-mannered reporter and there was a red cape sticking out from under his coat. The cook, dressed in a white T-shirt and cap, wiped the counter and poured coffee.

"I know what the problem is, Arthur," the Tick said as he dipped his tea bag in a cup of hot water. "I've spent over twenty minutes on patrol and I haven't found a single crime. This city is exceeding my attention span." He slurped his tea. "Why would they send a superhero of my caliber to a place like this? I'm not sure this city even needs a champion!"

Suddenly the unhappy man at the end of the counter spoke to the Tick. "So! You're a superhero, huh? And what sort of costume is that supposed to be?"

"Costume?" the Tick asked, a little confused. "No costume, friend. I am simply . . . the Tick."

"You can't be a tick!" the man argued. "Ticks are arachnids. They've got eight legs!"

The Tick retorted, "How do you know I don't?"

"Ticks suck blood," the man said. "Do you suck blood?"

The Tick eyed the cynical man. "Er . . . yeah . . . I—I suck blood all the time!"

"Yeah, right!" The cynic shook his head.

The Tick leapt to his feet and grabbed up a bendy straw. He glared at the man and said, "I got a straw right

12

here, pal! You want a demonstration?" The Tick stuck the straw in his mouth and made a long, scary sucking noise.

The cynical man backed away, smiling nervously. "Uh . . . no, thanks . . ."

Suddenly the quiet lunchtime discussion was disturbed by the sound of a powerful explosion. The Tick smiled. Arthur spun nervously on his stool.

"That's more like it!" the Tick cried, and ran out the door of the diner. "Come, Arthur! Evil is afoot!"

Arthur hesitated. "A—a foot? That's funny . . . I'd always pictured it as more of a dark, brooding shape with horns and claws."

"Adventure calls!" the Tick shouted as he reached back into the diner and yanked Arthur out.

Down the street they saw that someone had blown a hole in the side of a bank. They crept into an alley near the hole. They could see three men inside the bank. The men were wearing metal masks, carrying old-fashioned machine guns, and wearing nice sport coats that had little lightbulb patches sewn on the lapels. They were a criminal gang known as the Idea Men!

"This is definitely illegal," the Tick said. "Arthur, do you fly?"

"My wings are in my briefcase back at the diner." Arthur started to leave. "I'll go get them."

"No time, chum!" The Tick grabbed Arthur and leapt up onto the roof of the bank. Then they crashed through a skylight into the bank.

The three Idea Men turned in surprise at the sudden entrance of the Tick and Arthur. They pointed their guns at the heroic duo. Unfortunately, the Idea Men's masks didn't have holes for their mouths, so their threats were muffled.

Still, the sight of guns was too much for Arthur. "I think I'll just lie down here for a second." And he fainted.

"Criminals!" The Tick warned, "You face the sworn protector of this fair city. You face the Tick!"

The Idea Men mumbled something.

"Speak up!" the Tick said. "I can't understand a word you're saying through those stupid masks! Enunciate!"

Unknown to the Tick or the Idea Men, another of the City's many superheroes arrived on the scene. "This looks like a job for Crusading Chameleon!" said Crusading Chameleon. He was a man in a green outfit with suckers for toes and fingers. He had bulbous, reptilian eyes and his tongue flicked in and out like a snake's. He scuttled in through the skylight. As he crawled quickly along the wall, his costume changed to the color of the wall, making him difficult to see. He wanted to help the Tick catch the Idea Men, but when he reached the plaid curtains, his eyes started spinning. They were too difficult. He strained, "Can't . . . do . . . plaid!"

"Eat desk!" the Tick yelled as he threw a large wooden desk at the gun-toting Idea Men, knocking them to the ground. They scrambled to their feet and started running away.

Arthur stood up woozily. "Are we dead yet?"

"Far from it, Arthur!" the Tick said, beginning to chase the escaping Idea Men. "We have them on the run! Onward!"

The Idea Men rushed outside through the hole in the side of the bank. They weren't called the Idea Men for nothing. They had planned their escape brilliantly. Ropes dangled from above. They had a getaway blimp in the shape of a lightbulb floating over the bank. Each Idea Man grabbed a rope dangling from the blimp and it whisked them up into the sky over the City.

The Tick gazed at the escaping criminals and their airship.

"Hey, cool!" he said. "They've got a blimp!"

3

A Hero and His Sidekick
Face a Crisis

"That was the scene today at the Rive Droite Bank," said Sally Vacuum of Channel 17 News that night on television. They were showing footage of the Idea Men's attempted robbery and escape. "The mysterious gang known as the Idea Men struck again, continuing their terrible crime wave. It was the sixth time in as many days that the baffling criminals have descended from the sky to literally lift the City's most valued assets."

She turned to face another camera. "But today their nefarious plot was thwarted by a heroic blue stranger." The film showed the Tick emerging from the hole in the bank wall and saying, "Hey, cool! They've got a blimp!"

"Our modest blue benefactor exited the scene without comment. But the Idea Men menace is far from over, says Mayor Blank."

Then there was footage of Mayor Blank speaking at a press conference. "We have reason to believe," the Mayor said, "that these criminals were merely practicing for a much larger caper."

Sally Vacuum continued, "More on this story as it develops. Meanwhile, on a lighter note . . . clowns!"

The Tick and Arthur didn't see themselves on television. They arrived late at Arthur's modest apartment.

"This is my place," Arthur said as they entered. "What do you think?"

"It's great!" the Tick answered. "It looks just like an apartment! Where's your secret headquarters trigger? Is this it?" He yanked a coat hook off the wall.

"Oh, sorry." He handed the coat hook to a surprised Arthur. "You know, a trigger. A statue or a candlestick that you twist, and then everything flips over, and all your crime-busting equipment pops out!" The Tick grabbed a lamp. "Is this it?"

Arthur quickly leapt to rescue his favorite lamp. Then the Tick looked at the sofa.

"What does your sofa turn into? A sonar/radar perimeter defense unit?" The Tick flipped the sofa, knocking over books and spilling a cold cup of coffee that had been nearby.

"No! It turns into a bed!" Arthur was growing upset. "This is just an apartment!"

"It is?" The Tick was puzzled.

"Yes!" Arthur yelled.

The Tick began to think as Arthur sat down on the overturned sofa, holding his lamp tight.

The Tick said, "Well, this place is going to take a lot of work if it's going to be our superhero headquarters."

Arthur said quietly, "I don't know. I just don't know if I'm ready for this. Too much excitement! Too much adventure! I think I'm . . . going crazy!"

"You're not going crazy." The Tick smiled gently and patted Arthur's shoulder. "You're going sane in a crazy world! Some people are destined for greater things. You are one of those people. You can't hide from it! You've got to hug it! Hug your destiny, Arthur!"

The only thing that Arthur wanted to hug was his lamp. He said, "Uh-huh. I think I'll just sleep on it, okay?"

"That's fine, small friend," the Tick said. He picked up the TV remote control. "You rest up, and I will . . . monitor the culture!"

The Tick watched television. He was intrigued by a commercial for Drama Flakes cereal that insisted that "attractive, successful people loooove Drama Flakes! Guaranteed to make your life more dramatic and eventful with every golden spoonful!" The Tick clicked through the channels.

Suddenly he heard Sally Vacuum's voice. "Good evening, this is Sally Vacuum with a special report." On the screen the Tick saw the City Dam lit up by spotlights. Police cars were everywhere, their lights flashing red and blue. Above the dam floated the Idea Men's blimp. The camera panned down to show Sally Vacuum holding a microphone. "I'm here at the City's hydroelectric plant. Apparently, the notorious Idea Men have taken the City Dam hostage, although we can't understand a word they're saying."

There was video footage of one of the Idea Men on top

of the dam. He gestured wildly with his arms, but he was mumbling.

"What?" yelled Police Chief Louder through his bullhorn. "I'm sorry, we didn't get that."

Another Idea Man ran in and held up a sign that he had hastily written on a large piece of paper. It read: GIVE MONEY OR BOMB DAM FLOOD CITY!!!

"Good heavens!" the Tick exclaimed, leaping to his feet and running to Arthur's bedroom. "Arthur! Get up! The City calls upon her steadfast protectors!"

Arthur was asleep with his lamp. He muttered something sleepily. The next thing he knew he was on the roof, clutching his briefcase, with the Tick.

"Get those wings on, Arthur!" the Tick shouted.

"This isn't such a good idea," Arthur protested. "I'm not so good at this."

"You'll get better!" the Tick said.

"I've never flown before!" Arthur yelled in frustration.

The Tick stared at his friend. "Not a problem," he said confidently.

Moments later Arthur stood nervously on the edge of the roof. His big, mothlike wings were strapped to his back. The wind blew through his antennae. But Arthur wasn't sure he wanted to fly.

He yelled, "No, no, no, no, no!"

"It's your destiny, Arthur!" the Tick said firmly. "Hug it!"

He did. Arthur leapt off the roof and flapped his wings. And he flew.

"I'm very frightened," he yelled down at the Tick as he circled the apartment building.

"No, Arthur!" the Tick corrected him. "You're very flying! You see? No more doubting yourself!" The Tick pointed off heroically. "Now, on to the dam! We have work to do!"

The Tick bounded across the rooftops, followed by the fluttering Arthur. Suddenly the Tick stopped bounding. He stood at the edge of a building and looked. Far in the distance he could see the dam lit up and the Idea Men's blimp hovering over it. There was nothing but tree-filled countryside between the Tick and the far-off dam.

The Tick looked worried. "We're all out of roofs!"

4

The Value of a Good Education

The Tick and Arthur stood on the last roof at the edge of the City. They were trying to think of a superheroic way to get to the dam. Suddenly a metal batlike grappling hook connected to a steel cable whizzed past them and latched onto a nearby chimney. Then, sliding down the cable from another building came the mysterious caped hero, Die Fledermaus. He wore a dark costume, a long spooky cape, and a cowl with big bat ears. He landed on the roof next to the Tick and assumed a heroic pose.

"Out of roofs, eh?" Die Fledermaus said in a deep, scary voice.

Then another person yelled "Die Fledermaus!" from behind them.

They turned to see American Maid walking toward them. Her high-heeled shoes tapped on the tar-paper surface of the roof. She was dressed in a maid's outfit that seemed to have been sewn from an American flag. She looked like someone you shouldn't mess with unless you wanted to get your clock cleaned.

"I should've known you'd be out tonight!" she said to Die Fledermaus angrily.

"Well, if it isn't the world's most patriotic domestic!" Die Fledermaus snarled. "This looks like a job for Die Fledermaus! Not some mop squeezer! Why don't you go scrub out a toilet!"

American Maid eyed the mystery man viciously. "Why don't you go smell up a cave!"

The Tick raised his hands. "People! People! There's a dam about to be blown up! We should team up and use all our resources to battle this evil!"

But American Maid and Die Fledermaus continued to argue, paying no attention to the Tick.

The Tick turned to Arthur. "Some people shouldn't be in this business. To the dam!" The Tick leapt off the roof and Arthur flew after him.

As they left, another figure emerged from the shadows of the roof. He was a muscular man in a black costume and his belt buckle was a big skull emblazoned with the word *Good-bye*. He carried big guns, real big guns. "Amateurs!" he hissed. "None of them knows how to handle evil." He opened fire on the chimney nearby, blowing off bricks but not disturbing the two quarreling heroes. "This looks like a job for . . . Big Shot!"

The Tick and Arthur took a taxi to the dam. The Tick leapt out and began striding toward the dam, past the sign that read NO TRESPASSING—CITY PROPERTY. Arthur counted on his fingers, trying to figure out how much to tip the cab driver.

"Let's see," he calculated. "Fifteen percent of . . ." He looked up to see the Tick moving off quickly. He tossed the driver some money. "Just keep the change."

He caught up to the Tick just as the hero said, "Arthur! It's just occurred to me. We have no plan. And I know nothing about dams!"

"That's okay, Tick," Arthur said, gasping for breath. "I just . . . read a . . . whole book about them. For centuries man has harnessed the power of falling water. Today's hydroelectric facility converts the kinetic energy of running water into stored electrical power by controlling its flow. At the base of the City Dam, giant turbines generate the electricity that powers our homes and factories." Arthur smiled and pointed to the electric turbines in the distance. "If I were going to blow up the dam, that's where I'd put my bomb."

"Very thorough, Arthur," the Tick said. "Now back to action!" The two heroes made their way to the dark tunnels under the dam and quietly tiptoed inside. Then they saw the Idea Men mumbling in sinister tones in the gigantic chamber where the electric turbines hummed with power. The criminals had placed a bomb, encased in metal, on the turbines. Exactly as Arthur had said. The Idea Men were speaking on a walkie-talkie to the mayor and police chief outside. The Idea Men began to mumble happily. Arthur said, "They must have gotten the ransom money they wanted!"

Then one of the Idea Men reached for their bomb. He turned it on. It started beeping.

"Hey!" Arthur whispered angrily. "They got their money and they're still going to blow up the dam!"

"Aww—no fair!" the Tick complained.

Meanwhile, more of the City's superheroes responded to the dam crisis. The Human Bullet strapped on his cone-shaped steel helmet, raced out the back door of his suburban home, and climbed into the big cannon in his backyard. Turning to his son, he commanded, "Fire me, boy!" The cannon boomed and the Human Bullet shot in the direction of the dam. Across town, Bi-Polar Bear wanted to help, but he was too depressed to get out of bed. Mild-mannered reporter Rex Oppenheimer couldn't find a phone booth to change his clothes in. And Captain Lemming, using his unique powers, leapt off the roof of a high building and crashed to the ground. "Ouch!" he yelped. He had landed on his keys.

Back at the dam, the Tick had seen enough. He leapt from his hiding place. He landed with enough force to drive his feet into the concrete, starting a series of cracks in the floor that knocked the Idea Men off balance. The Tick picked one up by the lapels of his coat.

"Okay, Idea Man!" he yelled. "What's the big idea?"

The Idea Man's mask fell off and he said, "We thought we'd steal a lot of money so we'd be rich and wouldn't have to work anymore."

"You cads!" the Tick scolded. "Now turn off your bomb."

The Idea Men looked at each other. The one held by the Tick answered, "We can't. Once it's activated, it can't be shut off."

Tick dropped the Idea Man and grabbed the bomb. He looked at the smooth metal case for a minute. Then he smashed his hand into the bomb's side. Arthur covered his eyes.

"What are you doing?" Arthur murmured, peeking out from between his fingers.

"Shhh," the Tick whispered. He moved his hand around inside the bomb casing. "I'm defusing it." He slowly pulled out a handful of wires. The beeps came faster. Arthur covered his eyes. The Tick gently put his hand and the wires back into the bomb and the beeps got slow again.

The Idea Men quickly scrambled to their feet and ran off down a dark tunnel. Then, suddenly, the tunnel was filled with the sound of gunfire. A cloud of smoke blew out of the tunnel into the chamber where the Tick and Arthur were. Big Shot stepped into the chamber. A tear rolled down his cheek. He had missed them, every single escaping Idea Man. And now his guns were empty.

"Why didn't you love me, Mom?" Big Shot cried. He clearly had more problems than simply escaped criminals.

The Tick leaned toward Big Shot. "Seek professional help." Then he realized that the bomb was still ticking. "My goodness! I'm a walking time bomb! Get out of my way!"

The Tick raced past the sniffling Big Shot and into the tunnel. Arthur looked at Big Shot. Big Shot looked at Arthur, then crumpled into Arthur's arms, weeping.

The Tick ran out onto the top of the dam, carrying the ticking bomb in front of him. The Idea Men ran for their lives ahead of him. They jumped for the ropes that dangled from their blimp. The timer beeped down from :03 – :02 – :01 – :00. Then it pinged and the bomb exploded with a gigantic roar. A fireball engulfed the Idea Men's blimp, sending the criminals parachuting into the arms of the police.

When the smoke cleared, the Tick stood proud and tall, although a little blackened. Arthur raced up to him on the dam, relieved to see that his mighty friend was safe.

Arthur said, "Well, I guess we saved the City."

"For the moment, yes, my friend," the Tick proclaimed. "With luck, our future holds still more dire threats . . . more perilous plots. Wherever Villainy rears its great big head, wherever Evil sets its giant, ill-smelling foot, you will find the Tick. . . ."

The Tick smiled broadly, placing one powerful arm on Arthur's shoulder. When Arthur didn't say anything, he gave a quick squeeze.

"Oh," Arthur said. "And Arthur . . . his . . . uh . . . sidekick!"

"Good show! And my sidekick, Arthur! Certainly a force to be reckoned with." The Tick looked out over the wonderful City he was sworn to safeguard. "And so, may Evil beware! And may Good dress warmly and eat plenty of fresh vegetables!"

The only sound that could be heard through the still, safe night was the high-pitched whistling of the Human Bullet as he streaked through the sky, and a metallic thud as he slammed into the dam. The Human Bullet slid quietly into the water. His head would ache tomorrow.

Part 2

THE TICK
VS. THE
BREADMASTER

1

The Bread Is on Aisle Seven
. . . and Aisle Eight
. . . and . . .

"I'm not sure I approve of this interruption, Arthur," the Tick said. Arthur was wrestling a shopping cart free just inside the entrance of Stuart's Food Castle. "When we're on patrol, our first order of business must be the patrol."

Arthur moved off with his cart. "Tick, it'll just take a minute. If we don't do the shopping, we won't have anything for dinner."

"Very well, then. Shop away." The Tick narrowed his eyes and looked from side to side. "I will patrol the supermarket!"

The Tick moved stealthily, searching the aisles for crimes. "Hi. Would you care for a free sample?" The Tick looked down. A short man in a badly made suit and a milk carton head held out a tray with four glasses of milk on it. Next to him was a sign that read: MILKIE THE MILK BOY SAYS "DRINK IT DOWN!"

"I would indeed!" the Tick said. He took a glass and

gulped it down. "Ah, dairy goodness!" The Tick didn't notice that his calcium-fortified drink left a white milk moustache on his upper lip.

Not far away, Stuart, the owner of the store, noticed Arthur as the hero approached the deli counter. "Hey, Arthur," Stuart said with a friendly wave. "How's it going? You still a superhero?"

Arthur nodded. "Oh, yeah," he said casually.

The Tick walked up. "There you are, Arthur. Hello, Stuart!"

"Oh. Hey, Tick," said Stuart. He waved to the Tick as the phone on the counter rang. He answered it and heard a strange, sinister voice say, "Evacuate the building!" Stuart thought it was a joke. He answered calmly, "Uh-huh."

Arthur stared at the Tick's milk moustache. Not wanting to embarrass his mighty blue friend by calling a lot of attention to it, Arthur began wiping at his own mouth, hoping the Tick would get the hint. "Tick, you've got some . . . right here . . . a. . . ," he whispered.

"Gad!" the Tick exclaimed. "A Crumb? An errant particle? I am besmirched!" He wiped his hand over every part of his face except where the milk moustache was. "Did I get it?"

"No . . . no, Tick. Here." Arthur rubbed his face again.

"Uh-huh. Yeah, right. Sure . . . whatever you say, buddy." Stuart nodded and rolled his eyes at the voice on the other end of the line. He hung up the phone. The Tick and Arthur looked at him.

Stuart said, "Some guy calling himself the Breadmaster. Said he planted a loaf of bread in the building. And it's set to go off at noon."

Arthur looked at his watch. "Well, it's almost noon now."

Stuart shrugged and went back to filling Arthur's order for a half pound of Swiss cheese. Suddenly they heard a rumble and the floor started to shake. Shoppers began screaming. When the Tick and Arthur quickly turned, they saw an incredibly gigantic loaf of bread pushing its way out of the cellar. It knocked over shelves as it expanded onto the floor of the market. The other end of the loaf grew toward the door. When it reached the exit, it squeezed through and smashed the swinging doors off their hinges. The walls of the store began to crack from the strain caused by the expanding loaf.

"Hey," Stuart said with shock. "That's . . . that's bread!"

The Tick yelled, "Run, Stuart, while you still can! There's evil on the rise."

The bread surged upward, reaching the twenty-foot ceiling and smashing the fluorescent light fixtures. The building's steel support beams began to twist with a wrenching sound.

The Tick ran toward the monster bread. He reached the center aisle and stared down it. The bread was heading his way fast.

The Tick pointed and called out, "Yeast beast! Back to the oven that baked you!" He rushed at the doughy colossus.

Arthur joined the Tick on the center aisle. "I've got a terrible headache."

As the Tick raced toward the pulsating bread, he saw himself in a glass-front display case. "Milk moustache!" he yelled in alarm, and wiped his face properly.

Then the Tick attacked the monster bread, punching it with his powerful fist. *"Phup!"* His arm sank deep into the warm, doughy loaf and he could not pull it out! "Good heavens!" he exclaimed. The bread continued to move and expand, sucking the Tick in deeper. It lurched forward, growing farther, until the heel of the loaf pressed against his shocked and straining face.

"Arthur! Save yourself!" he called to his faithful side-kick. The Tick took one last gasp of air before his face was swallowed by bread. Only one of his blue arms remained outside.

"Hang on, Tick!" Arthur yelled out. He picked up a rolling pin, but the bread had gotten far too large for that. It was swallowing everything in its path. Arthur glanced around wildly. The Big Dunker Waterproof Donuts display! He threw down the rolling pin and ran to the pyramid of boxed donuts atop which sat a giant 3-D donut. He took the big plastic donut off the top. Then he grabbed a clothesline from the housewares aisle and tied it to the big donut.

Inside the bread, it was warm and soft. It made the Tick sleepy. He wanted to sleep forever. But then he heard Arthur's voice calling, "Fight it, Tick! Don't go under!"

"Yes!" the Tick said to himself. "Must . . . resist!" He shook his head, trying to wake up. "Must not . . . succumb . . . to the rapture of the bread!"

Arthur threw the donut life preserver at the bread and the Tick's hand shot out and grabbed it. Using his mighty strength, the Tick surged free of the quivering bread and he took a breath of air.

"Good show, Arthur," the Tick called out. "You've given me another shot at this thing called life!"

Arthur tied the other end of the clothesline to a cash register and rubbed the bridge of his nose. His headache was getting worse.

The Tick heard a noise from deep inside the bread. He listened intently and yelled, "Arthur!" Then he dove back into the gooey mass. In seconds he returned to the surface holding a beagle puppy. "Puppy!" he shouted in triumph. He tossed the dog to Arthur, who guided it to the front door and freedom.

The Tick pulled himself completely free of the bread. The gargantuan loaf slammed against the ceiling again, pushing it up. The Tick stood for a minute watching the bread approach him. It was pulsing, breathing like a living thing!

"I'm afraid it's a bust, Arthur!" the Tick said to his already retreating sidekick. "Save what you can!" He grabbed several items off the shelves as he and Arthur ran for the door.

Out in the parking lot, Stuart stood with a crowd of people watching as the Tick and Arthur escaped the loaf of bread that had demolished his store. The bread moved to within feet of the crowd, then rumbled and stopped growing. The Tick took a hunk and popped it into his mouth. "Huh! That's quite good!"

Arthur tried to comfort Stuart. "It must be a terrible shock."

"I'll say," Stuart answered sadly. "I don't have bread insurance."

The Tick was still wearing his giant donut life preserver around his waist. "Don't despair, Stuart. You can rebuild! Start with these!" He handed Stuart a package that he had saved from the store. "Cottony swabs!"

2

A Recipe for Evil

In an old abandoned bakery in the dark, decaying heart of the City's warehouse district, the Breadmaster picked up the phone and dialed a number. The Breadmaster was a tall, thin man who wore a black baker's apron and black chef's hat. He was a master baker, creating evil breads and cakes as if by magic.

"Is this the Whitebread Baking Company?" he asked into the phone. "This is the Breadmaster, with a question for you. Have you no shame? Have you no decency? Can you not cry for the millions victimized by your barbarism? Because of you, the masses know *nothing* of *real* bread!" The Breadmaster continued to fill baking pans with dough as he talked. "Oh, yes, I've sampled that pallid, flavorless sponge you peddle. It sticks to the roof of my mouth! It rolls eagerly between thumb and forefinger into hard, tasteless pellets!" He listened for a second. "*Yes,* I want to register a complaint! Your bread is a disgrace!"

The Breadmaster turned to place a muffin pan into the oven. He watched the flames licking the inside of the oven, the heat pouring out over him. "Hear me, perpetrators of bread crime—your punishment is at hand! I have planted in your factory a loaf of self-baking bread. When the clock strikes four, it will detonate!"

The Breadmaster hung up the phone and looked at the clock. It read 3:59. His henchman, Buttery Pat, smiled a greasy smile at him. Buttery Pat was a round, oily guy. He had a large square of melting butter on top of his head and liquid butter oozed from his hands and feet. He started to butter a loaf of bread with his fingers.

Across town, the Tick and Arthur were continuing their patrol. The Tick leapt from rooftop to rooftop while Arthur flapped after him using his moth wings.

"I must say, little chum," the Tick said, "your instincts are improving. Stopping at Stuart's proved more heroic than I anticipated."

Arthur wasn't sure. "Some heroism. The place was demolished!"

The Tick smiled. "Details, Arthur! You're obsessing again!"

Just then, the Tick leapt from the edge of a rooftop and landed on top of a giant loaf of bread rising from below. The Tick glanced down, mildly surprised. "Hmmm. More bread."

Arthur fluttered down to land next to him. The Tick bent down and tore off a piece of the bread. He sniffed it and then ate it. "You know," he said while chewing, "I think this loaf came from the same guy."

* * *

Meanwhile, the gooey Buttery Pat made his way through the City. He slid along streets using the butter from his feet, leaving greasy skid marks behind him. He skated into an alley that ran beside the City Baking College, where all of the City's greatest bakers learned their skills. He schussed to a stop in front of a window like a skier, throwing up a wave of butter that splashed onto the wall and oozed down. Nobody saw Pat as he quietly squeezed his oily body through the metal bars that protected one of the windows and slipped inside the college. He was carrying a suspicious loaf of bread!

Arthur spotted something from their perch on top of the giant loaf of bread. Police cars surrounded the loaf and the pile of rubble at its base that had once been a factory. Long strands of tape reading POLICE LINE—DO NOT CROSS kept the curious away from the bread.

"Tick, look!" Arthur cried, pointing to a smashed sign below. The sign showed a tender family scene: two blond children were biting into slices of white bread while their parents watched with adoring smiles, obviously pleased that their children were enjoying the doughy treat. Arthur read the caption on the sign: THE WHITEBREAD BAKING COMPANY.

The Tick leapt onto a nearby building and stroked his mighty chin in thought. "So this guy's a baker, and he's evil."

"Who would know about evil bakers?" Arthur asked.

"I know! The City Baking College!"

The dean of the baking college showed the Tick and Arthur through the college. He wore the long black robe preferred by professors and a tall white baker's hat on his head. They walked down the dark Hall of Strange Baking Oddities, which contained display cases with unusual items like the misshapen Wisconsin Cruller Man. The Tick and Arthur were mildly frightened by the weirdness.

The dean said, "I've been dean here for over twenty-five years, and in all that time I had only one student with enough skill to devise bread bombs like the one you describe. In fact, that student was expelled from this very institution."

"Why?" asked Arthur.

"For pursuing perverse baking experiments," the dean answered as they walked into his office. "Flagrant violations of the baker's code. Projectile Danish, floating pies—that sort of thing. He baked a muffin that stole my car! He left here in disgrace. I haven't heard from him since." The dean's phone rang and he answered it. "Hello?"

"Remember me, Dean?" asked a sinister voice on the phone. "I am the Breadmaster and I remember you! You who denied me my baking license! And why? Because your tiny ego couldn't withstand the threat of my culinary genius. Well, today at exactly five o'clock your tyranny ends!"

Suddenly one of the college's baking professors rushed into the dean's office in a panic. "Dean!" he yelled. "A loaf of bread has been found in the basement!"

"Can I call you back?" the dean said to the Breadmaster. "We have a situation here." He hung up the phone, leaving the Breadmaster snarling with anger back in his bakery.

Then the dean led the Tick and Arthur into the dark basement where the scary bread lay in wait.

3

Stir in 637 Cups of Sugar

Back in the deepest, darkest corner of the basement, hidden among the discarded cookie jars, baking pans, and rolling pins, sat a loaf of bread that didn't belong there.

"There!" the baking professor shouted. "Examine it yourself and tell me we're not dealing with suspicious baked goods."

"Not baked goods," the Tick said. "Baked bads!" He quickly dropped to one knee and examined the loaf carefully. "Time?"

Arthur looked at his watch. "Four fifty-nine . . . and ten seconds!"

"Hmmm," the Tick said. "Fifty seconds to defuse a loaf of bread. Not good." The Tick eyed the loaf. Then he plunged his hand deep into it. The dean and the professor both gasped. The Tick listened to the bread.

"Thirty seconds!" Arthur called.

"Bread knife!" the Tick commanded, extending his

hand back. The professor grabbed an old knife from a nearby crate and gave it to the Tick. The Tick put down the bread and carefully cut a slice off the end. Beads of sweat dripped down his face.

"Ten seconds!" Arthur said. Then, "Five!"

The loaf of bread began to rumble. The Tick's eyes widened in alarm. "Evacuate the building!" he yelled. "This bread's going to blow!"

Arthur shoved the frightened dean and professor out of the basement. When he turned back around, the Tick was pressing the loaf between his two superstrong hands, trying to keep it from growing. The bread bubbled and bucked, trying to free itself from the Tick's grip. He gritted his teeth, straining with all his powerful strength to control the rebellious loaf.

"Wait a minute!" the Tick exclaimed with a sudden smile. He wrestled the entire loaf of bread up to his mouth, shoved it in, and swallowed it whole! Arthur stared in frightened amazement.

Then the Tick's stomach began to rumble. "Good heavens!" he said. "What have I done?" The Tick's midsection began to expand. The bread was still growing, even inside the Tick's superstrong stomach! The Tick punched his moving stomach, trying to defeat the unruly meal. After a minute of struggle, the bread was quiet.

"You did it!" Arthur shouted. "You ate that bread into submission!"

"This villainous baker means business," the Tick said. Then he covered his mouth and gave a little burp.

In that moment of triumph and stomach upset, they didn't see Buttery Pat, who crouched at the basement window watching the whole thing. He leapt to his greasy feet and slid back to his master.

"The Tick did *what*?" the Breadmaster yelled when Pat told him the news. "I should've known that sooner or later a superhero would get involved." The Breadmaster was very angry. He stalked to the telephone. "The times have become desperate. Which calls for desperate measures. Big—*very* big measures!" He punched a number into the phone. "Get me the mayor's office!" he said, and grinned a nasty grin.

From the Channel 17 News anchor desk, Sally Vacuum said, "And this so-called Breadmaster has issued an ultimatum to Mayor Blank. He's demanded common baking ingredients in enormous quantities." They showed video footage of a transfer truck pulling four long trailers. The trailers were labeled FLOUR, EGGS, MILK, and SUGAR. The Breadmaster was driving the truck. He waved at the camera. "And if they are not delivered," Sally continued, "per his instructions, he will escalate his bread bombings. Mayor Blank announced his decision at a press conference earlier today."

The Tick sat on the couch with Arthur. They could barely hear the news on television over the fizzing noise when the Tick dumped a whole bottleful of large white antacid tablets into a bucket of water. They watched the television as the smiling Mayor Blank said, "I've okayed the delivery of the supplies the Breadmaster demands."

A reporter yelled, "But, Your Honor, isn't it the City's policy to refuse all terrorist demands?"

"Yes, I suppose you could call these terrorist acts. But they're also acts of baking. Very fast, very big baking."

When the Tick gave a particularly loud belch, Arthur asked, "Are you okay?"

"I have to be, chum," the Tick answered. "We have much important work ahead of us! When this base baker gets to the sugar, he'll find the bitter taste of justice!"

It was early evening and the Breadmaster was driving an 18-wheeler with a trailer marked SUGAR. Buttery Pat sat on the seat beside him. Between them was a picnic basket full of exploding dinner rolls. The Breadmaster drove into the City sugar refinery and parked beneath the sugar silo, waiting for his truck to be filled. This was his last stop. He already had all of his flour, eggs, and milk.

Suddenly the Tick and Arthur leapt from hiding. The Tick pointed at the villain. "Breadmaster! Your culinary crime-wave has crashed against the shores of justice!" Arthur looked at his partner with admiration, impressed.

The Breadmaster stepped from the truck, carrying his picnic basket. "So, vermin, we meet at last!" He pulled a roll from the basket as Pat raced to his side. "Butter me, Pat!" the Breadmaster commanded. Pat dripped some butter from his head onto the roll. The Breadmaster bit a chunk from the roll, like a soldier pulling the pin of a grenade with his teeth, and threw it at the heroes.

The Tick and Arthur looked up in bewilderment as a large and rapidly growing shadow loomed over them. "Heads up, Arthur!" the Tick yelled, starting to back up. "Incoming roll!" The roll grew to the size of a boulder, then the size of a refrigerator. Then it landed on Arthur.

"Hang on, little chum!" cried the Tick.

"Tick! Help!" Arthur shouted. "Get this dinner roll off me!"

The Tick grabbed the large roll and lifted it off Arthur. The he hurled it back at the villain. The roll struck the Breadmaster and knocked him down.

Arthur held his head. "Too stressful . . . it's just too stressful."

As the Tick turned to leap after the two criminals, Buttery Pat sprayed the ground with a stream of superslick butter. The Tick began to slip and slide. He lost his footing and fell with a splat into the butter. Arthur tried to stand up and slithered helplessly.

"Gads!" the Tick exclaimed as he strained to move in the butter. "They're giving us the slip!"

The Breadmaster lobbed another bread grenade at the Tick and Arthur. He laughed as he climbed back into the truck. Buttery Pat was waiting for him in the cab. They started the truck and drove away.

Arthur had just gotten to his feet when the big roll landed on his head, driving him to the ground. He and the roll skidded through the ooze. The roll kept growing, expanding over the Tick, too, as he lay foundering in the butter. The soft bread puffed out over Arthur's head. He was going to be smothered!

"Persevere, embattled sidekick," the Tick urged. He grabbed the roll and began to pry it apart. "We'll break this bread yet!"

The Tick tore the roll wide enough for Arthur to sit up. He drew in lungfuls of air. Suddenly he said, "My wings!" and pressed the button on his chest that controlled his new moth-wings backpack. There was a high-pitched whining as the hydraulics of Arthur's backpack struggled to expand the wings against the weight of the surrounding dinner roll. Finally the wings sprang out, tearing the bread open like knives. He and the Tick fell back with relieved sighs.

"Hey, look!" Arthur pointed off in the distance. Sitting on the ground was the Breadmaster's picnic basket. "They must've dropped it."

The Tick and Arthur managed to get to their feet. They looked into the basket. "More rolls," said the Tick.

"And this," said Arthur. He pulled out a piece of paper that had a soufflé recipe written on it. He read the title aloud with growing amazement: "The Breadmaster's City-Smothering Lemon Dessert Soufflé."

The recipe began:

2,000 Cubic Feet Whole Milk
Yolks of 30,000 Gross of Eggs
6 Tons Granulated Sugar
4 Tons Flour
2 Tons Fresh Lemon Juice (Strained)
756 Lbs. Grated Lemon Rind
Whites of 50,000 Gross of Eggs
1 Boxcar Confectioners' Sugar for Dusting
     (Optional)
Step 1: Set aside 750 cubic feet of milk. . . .

This would be a gigantic soufflé, perhaps the largest the world had ever seen.

Arthur calculated the size of the recipe quietly. "Divide

by two hundred, carry the three." His eyes widened. "Oh, no! If I understand the proportions correctly, when a soufflé that big rises, it'll swallow the whole city!" He grabbed the picnic basket and raced for the gate of the sugar refinery. The Tick followed, flagging down a passing City bus.

As the bus pulled up, Arthur mused, "But where could he mix ingredients in that quantity? A large, enclosed space . . . like a stadium? Or a skating rink? Or . . ."

Then Arthur realized: "The Municipal Swimming Pool!"

4

The Soufflé That Conquered the World

Arthur was right. At the Municipal Swimming Pool, the Breadmaster was mixing his diabolical dish. He was standing up in a motorboat, dumping truckloads of flour and eggs and milk into the pool. Then he began to mix it by riding around the pool in the motorboat. Buttery Pat stood on the edge of the pool pouring in the last of the flour.

The Breadmaster said, "I suppose I should regret that we had to leave the sugar behind. But I'll still have my revenge on the City. And it will be just as sweet!"

"All right, Breadmaster!" The voice of the Tick suddenly boomed out from the high diving board. "That'll be about enough of that!" The Tick bounced once on the diving board and came off into a perfect swan dive, then a jackknife, then a triple twist, then a somersault, and finally a cannonball.

The Breadmaster's eyes widened in fear and he leapt

onto the side of the pool just as the Tick crashed straight into the boat, smashing it to pieces and splashing into the white, frothy dough. Then he surfaced in a geyser of batter, landing softly with a squish on the side of the pool near the Breadmaster.

He pointed at the villain. "Chef of chicanery! Your buns are mine!"

The Breadmaster and Buttery Pat started running. Arthur swooped in over them. He had one of the Breadmaster's exploding dinner rolls in his hand. "Rolls away!" he called as he dropped the roll onto the two fleeing criminals.

Buttery Pat tried to avoid the already expanding falling roll, but his feet were too slippery. He fell down, bounced off a wall, and collided with the Breadmaster, knocking them both down. As they tried to stand up, the Tick grabbed them in his powerful grip.

The Tick said, "You'll have much time to hone your baking skills in the prison mess hall." The police arrived and took the villains.

As he was taken off, the Breadmaster smirked at the Tick. "Perhaps, but you're too late to stop my self-baking soufflé!" He pointed at the pool, where the dough was beginning to pulse and grow. "Already it rises!"

Arthur gasped. "It'll smother the City! We've got to do something!"

"More thinking!" the Tick exclaimed. "We are well challenged, small friend!"

"Actually, a loud noise would . . ." Arthur paused and got an idea. "That's it! A sonic boom! It was discovered by Chuck Yeager, the first man to achieve level flight at Mach

1 speed. The sonic boom is a violently loud noise caused by the shock wave generated by an aircraft flying faster than the speed of sound! Though not harmful to humans or animals, a sonic boom can be, on some occasions, loud enough to shatter glass. And certainly enough to ruin a giant soufflé. But how to *cause* one?"

"Human Bullet . . . pssst . . . Bullet!" The Tick stood outside the bedroom window of the City's popular projectile personality. "Get up! It's an emergency!"

The Human Bullet sat up in bed. He was wearing pajamas and his metal bullet helmet. His eyes were puffy. He looked at the window. "What? Who's there?"

"Bullet! It's the Tick! Wake up! A huge soufflé is about to consume the City and we need your cannon!"

The Human Bullet threw back the covers. "Okay, okay." He yawned. "Let me put on some pants."

In the backyard, the Human Bullet led the Tick and Arthur to his big cannon, which he used to shoot himself to crime scenes.

Arthur explained, "We need a sonic boom to make the soufflé fall!"

The Tick instructed, "I want you to double—no, triple—the explosive charge you usually use!"

The Human Bullet jumped. "A triple charge! No! The explosion alone, not to mention the speed it would generate, could finish a normal human being!"

The Tick climbed into the mouth of the cannon. "Aha! The Tick is no normal human!"

The Human Bullet cringed and fired the cannon. The blast woke up the neighborhood. The Tick shot out of the cannon and blasted across the City at an altitude of one hundred feet. He streaked past with incredible speed, glowing brightly, turning night into day as he passed. A rolling thunderclap followed in his wake. Dogs barked as he screamed past overhead. His antennae were pressed flat against his head by the wind, and the G-forces of acceleration stretched his mouth wide.

The killer soufflé had grown rapidly, threatening to submerge the City at any moment in a cholesterol-filled invasion of rich, creamy batter. The Tick streaked over the soufflé and beyond the horizon. There followed the sharp, resounding crack of the sonic boom that his superfast flight had caused. The soufflé shuddered. The top of it exploded into a flurry of airy flakes and shreds. Underneath, it collapsed, crumbling and caving in on itself. It spread out, settling on buildings and homes. It coated the City with a sticky but harmless rainfall of pudding.

Later that night, the Tick and Arthur watched the gooey mess ooze away into the pool drain. The Tick wiped underdone soufflé off his costume.

"Well," Arthur said. "It looks like you've averted yet another threat to the City."

The Tick smiled. "Yes, and the City looks almost peaceful under a blanket of freshly fallen soufflé. But let us not forget the lesson we can learn from this." The Tick raised a stern finger. "Man was not meant to tamper with any of the four basic food groups!" Then he tasted the soufflé on his finger.

"Hmmm. Could use a little sugar."

Part 3

THE TICK VS. CHAIRFACE CHIPPENDALE

1

An Invitation to Crime

A full moon hung low over the City. It was bright and menacing. Luckily for the citizens of this fair town two superheroes were on patrol, searching for evil and foul play. The Tick and Arthur moved across the moonlit city-scape. The Tick leapt from rooftop to rooftop, leaving a trail of crumbling mortar and falling bricks. Arthur fluttered along behind him, held aloft by his strange and wonderful moth wings.

Arthur said, panting, "So, how much longer do we do this?"

The Tick landed on a swaying chimney and answered, "Well, we're on patrol. Hup!" He bounded to the next building. "So we patrol until something happens. A crime or something. Ho!"

Arthur drifted in the wind as the Tick leapt. "I mean, we've been patrolling for three hours. What if nothing happens?"

The Tick looked at his sidekick. "Arthur, we're *super-heroes*. Something *always* happens!"

The sound of a burglar alarm shattered the silence. The Tick smiled happily and leapt off in the direction of the alarm with Arthur flapping along behind him.

On the corner of Second Avenue and Maple Street, three shadowy figures were coming out of the Deadly Superweapons Laboratory's side entrance into a dark alley. They were members of the City's criminal underworld and they were up to no good. The man in front was called the Forehead. He was short and thin, dressed in a very nice gangster suit. And he had an unusually large forehead. A very unusually large forehead. The other two were big, strong, goonish types. The first was Boils Brown, over six feet tall and covered with big, unsightly bumps. The other was called Zipperneck. He was a giant of a man, nearly seven feet tall, with a zipper sewn into his neck. Boils Brown and Zipperneck were carrying a large wooden crate between them.

The Forehead listened to the clanging alarm. "Boils! Zipperneck! That bell's giving me a headache," he said. "Let's get out of here."

Before the three evildoers could move, their path was blocked by the Tick. He towered above them atop a Dumpster at the end of the alley. He commanded, "Not so fast, naughty spawn! You face the Tick! I say to you: Stop your evil ways!"

The larcenous trio stared up at him in momentary surprise. Then they started laughing. The Tick was taken aback. Above him, Arthur hovered, waiting for the Tick to make his move.

Crouching on a rooftop above Arthur, American Maid drummed her fingers with annoyance. "Big blue jerk!" she said to herself. "He's going to ruin everything!" She was another of the City's superfolk and she knew the Tick from when the Idea Men tried to blow up the City Dam. She had been waiting on the roof to pounce on the Forehead and his boys when the Tick suddenly showed up.

The Forehead stopped laughing and said to the Tick, "Look, fella, you can play pajama police all you want. Just remember who you're dealing with."

"Yeah," said Boils. "We run this town!"

"Yeah," said Zipperneck, "we're the . . ." He paused to think. "We're the curdled cream of the criminal crop. Right, boss?"

"Nicely put," the Forehead commented. He was a criminal who appreciated a well-turned phrase. "And you can bank on that, bug boy!"

At the Forehead's last words, the Tick jumped off the Dumpster and grabbed the Forehead by his coat lapels and jerked him up to eye level. "You're in a lot of trouble, mister!"

The Forehead yelled, "Zipperneck! Show him your stuff!"

Zipperneck ran up so the Tick could see him better. He reached up and unzipped the hole in his neck. "Hey! Look at this!"

"Oh, *gross!*" The Tick dropped the Forehead and covered his eyes. Zipperneck gave the Tick a mighty shove. The hero went sailing into the side of the Dumpster.

The Tick looked up and said, "So, *that's* the way you want it, eh?"

The Tick and Zipperneck started fighting. Arthur watched in dismay, then tried to help. He landed next to the big crate where the Forehead and Boils Brown stood watching the scuffle.

"Who are you?" the Forehead asked.

Arthur stammered, "Uh . . . I—I'm the sidekick."

The Forehead nodded. "Okay." He snapped his fingers. "Boils! Kick him in the side!"

Arthur backed away from the gigantic Boils, saying, "I don't think we're past the point of discussion."

Across the alley, the Tick socked Zipperneck so hard that the brawny crook flew back into the wall with a thud. Zipperneck wasn't badly hurt, but he was surprised. "Ow . . . ?" he said as he looked around for something big and heavy to hit the Tick with.

"See what you made me do!" the Tick shouted. "Not so funny, is it?"

Zipperneck reached up and twisted a fire escape off the side of the building with a wrenching, creaking sound. Then he stuffed it over the Tick and began to wrap it around the hero. The Tick grunted, his eyes bugging out.

The Tick flexed his muscles and yanked one arm loose. He reached out and plucked a stop sign out of the sidewalk. And then he bopped Zipperneck with it.

On the rooftop above, American Maid decided to help the heroes. She leapt off the roof, yelling her famous battle cry, "Time to clean house!"

The Forehead quickly pried open the big wooden crate and removed a briefcase from inside. Then he began to run. American Maid landed with catlike grace and quickly slipped off one of her fashionable high-heeled shoes. Just as she was about to throw it at the escaping Forehead, she heard Arthur cry for help. Turning around, she saw Boils about to grab Arthur. She launched her shoe at Boils with deadly accuracy. The heel of the shoe pierced Boil's jacket and stuck into the wall—*thunk!*—pinning him there like a big, ugly butterfly in a bug collection.

The Tick chased Zipperneck farther into the alley.

The Forehead came out of the alley onto the street. He was panting as he looked both ways. Then he took off at a dead run, clutching the metal briefcase tightly.

Boils Brown grunted as he tugged at the shoe that held him to the wall. American Maid launched herself in a flying tackle that took Boils by surprise. She drove him into the wall and knocked him unconscious.

The Tick chased Zipperneck back out toward the front of the alley.

American Maid looked at Arthur. He was a little woozy. She asked, "Are you all right?"

"Yes, thanks," he answered. "You certainly helped out."

Hands on hips, she glared at Arthur with a disapproving scowl. "Well, you and your friend didn't help me much! You've ruined a night's work!"

Zipperneck sailed past her and crashed into the wall next to Boils Brown. He slid down to the ground in a dazed heap. The Tick bounded up to American Maid and Arthur, triumphantly dusting his hands.

He said, "Ah! American Maid! Good of you to join us in yet another sterling victory over the forces of evil."

She reached up and grabbed one of the Tick's antennae, pulling his head down. "Listen, you blue goon—"

"Agh!" the Tick cried. "Careful! These things are sensitive."

American Maid spoke slowly. "I was *following* the Forehead and his boys. They would have led me to the Criminal Mastermind behind their wicked scheme. But *you* two messed that up, thank you very much!"

On the ground Arthur saw a piece of paper that had fallen out of Boils Brown's pocket. He picked it up and handed it to American Maid. She read it and said, "It's an invitation to a birthday party for the Criminal Mastermind. At the party he's going to commit the crime of the century!"

The Tick said, "Cool! The crime of the century!"

American Maid studied the invitation. Then she saw the embossed seal of the sender. It was a simple straightback chair in a circle. Her eyes grew wide. "I should've known. *Chippendale!*"

"Um . . . what's Chippendale?" Arthur asked.

"Not what. *Who.*" American Maid looked worried. Any criminal named for the most famous furniture in the world was going to be big trouble. "And he's too powerful for me to fight alone. I'm going to need some help."

The Tick cleared his throat. American Maid stared past him. The Tick flexed his muscles and cleared his throat louder.

American Maid turned to look at him. She sighed, "Oh, all right. I guess I could do worse."

"Neat!" the Tick exclaimed.

American Maid's eyes narrowed. "Okay. Now, here's the plan. . . ," she began.

2

The Perfect Birthday Present

A long, black limousine approached the isolated mansion fortress of Chairface Chippendale. The mansion sat high above a river on a mountainous crag. Emerging from the limo was the Forehead. He had brought the stolen briefcase with him. He knocked three times on the huge wooden doors and listened as the sound echoed through the mansion. One of the doors creaked open and the Forehead saw a very tall figure with hooks for hands. It was Hooks Horowitz, the doorman. The Forehead was escorted through the long, dark halls to a room where he met Professor Chromedome, Chippendale's mad-scientist assistant. Professor Chromedome was bald and hunched over. He wore a lab coat and goggles and had a mad-scientist grin.

His voice even had a mad-scientist accent. "Ah! Ze Forehead. Und vhere iss your pahtners in crime?"

The Forehead smiled. "*They* got nabbed. But *I* got the goods." He lifted the briefcase and shook it.

"Ach! Dummkopf!" Professor Chromedome screamed with a horrified look. "Don't shake it!" Chromedome grabbed the briefcase and clutched it tightly. "How can you haff zuch a bick head und zuch a tiny brain?" The professor then walked through two large doors into a fancy room with a fire crackling in the fireplace. The Forehead followed him. Chromedome approached a man sitting in an armchair turned toward the fire. "Herr Chippendale, ve haff ze lenze."

"The Geismann lens?" Chippendale asked. "Let's take a look at it, shall we?" He removed from the briefcase a clear crystal lens that looked like the lens of a magnifying glass. It sparkled brightly as it caught the firelight and a beam of light shot out of the lens and burned the Forehead.

The Forehead yelled and Chromedome said, "Yesss! Zeese babies can really burn! Vhen properly set, zey can focus ze light of a zingle candle into a heat ray of unparalleled power!"

Chairface Chippendale stood up to reveal his true appearance. He was a well-dressed, normal-sized man, but he had a wooden chair for a head! "It's just what I need to complete my superweapon. Now I ask you, is this a birthday present or what?" Chippendale's evil laughter echoed through the huge mansion.

Meanwhile, the Tick and Arthur waited on a street corner.

"What's keeping American Maid?" Arthur asked nervously. "She said she'd meet us at five."

The Tick heard the scraping sound of a manhole cover

being shoved aside. He looked down to see a superhero wearing a dark purple wet suit covered with spines trying to climb out of the manhole. Unfortunately, the hero's scuba tank was too big to fit through the hole.

The Tick pointed. "Hey! It's Sewer Urchin! How are you today?"

"Poisonous," Sewer Urchin answered. "So don't touch me."

"Ho ho!" the Tick laughed good-naturedly. "Who'd want to?"

The Sewer Urchin weaved and bobbed, shadowboxing. "You guys got any superaction going on up there? Any supervillains you need a hand with?"

Arthur said, "Yeah, we're going to stop the crime of the cen—"

The Tick interrupted Arthur by picking him up and putting him down several feet away. "Ixnay on the anplay. Okay?" the Tick whispered to Arthur. American Maid hadn't asked for any other heroes on this caper. The Tick said to Sewer Urchin, "No, no, its pretty quiet up here. See you later."

Sewer Urchin was suspicious. "Yeah. Right." He eyed the Tick as he slid back under the manhole cover. Just as he pulled it shut a caterer's van with a large fiberglass croissant on top of it rolled to a stop on top of the manhole cover.

"Get in, boys!" American Maid yelled from the driver's seat. She tossed them white waiter's outfits. "Here, put these on. We're going to sneak into Chippendale's party as caterers."

"The Tick caters to no man!" the Tick proclaimed, striking a pose.

She sighed. "Work with me here, will you?"

3

Villains, Alligators, and a Man-Eating Cow

As the heroes raced toward destiny, Chippendale's mountaintop fortress was already full of the worst criminals and villains the world had ever seen; it was a menagerie of wrongdoers, a buffet of bad guys. There was the Crease, Harriet Curse, Headless Henderson, the Guy with Ears like Little Raisins, Sheila Eel, Jack Tuber, and Eyebrows Mulligan. The Ugly Mugs and the Deadly Nose were also there. And they each brought a nice gift for the rottenest birthday boy ever—Chairface Chippendale.

Chippendale sat on a throne. He looked dully at a present he had just unwrapped. It was a boxful of diamonds. "Oh. Diamonds. How original." He dropped them carelessly onto a pile of fabulous loot next to his chair. "More gifts!"

The bizarre Guy Who Looks Just like Peter Lorre stepped up and handed Chippendale one end of a long red ribbon. The other end was attached to a muscular thug who had a big metal wing nut for a head. "Happy birthday, Chairface. I hope you like it. He's the Butterfly Nutcase, my best henchman. He has the strongest hands in the criminal world."

The Butterfly Nutcase grabbed a diamond from the pile of loot. He squeezed it until it gave out a glassy screech. Then it imploded in a shower of diamond dust.

The guests gasped in delight. Chairface said, "I like *him*!"

Professor Chromedome stepped up and handed Chippendale a remote control. "Herr Chippendale, your veapon ist completed."

"Now, *this* is a gift!" Chippendale held up the remote control. "Ladies and gentlemen, with this deadly superweapon I will carve my name into the annals of history!"

American Maid's catering van raced through the gate and screeched up to the front door of the fortress. The heroes jumped out, ready to serve justice—and food. The Tick and Arthur were now dressed as waiters. The Tick was eating little pastries off a tray. "Yum. These crab things are great!" he said as they rushed inside with the food.

Chippendale announced to his guests, "And now—drinks and hors d'oeuvres!" just as the Tick burst into the large room, carrying a big silver platter of crab puffs. He shoved through the villains, spilling their drinks and knocking them aside.

"Hors d'oeuvres!" he called. "Hors d'oeuvres!"

Arthur entered the room with his tray of food. "Would

anyone care for a—" A sudden barrage of villainous hands descended on his tray. He was picked clean in a flash. Arthur was appalled by the horrendous slurping and chewing around him. "Hey! Where'd you people grow up?" he said.

The Tick shoved the tray at the Guy with Ears like Little Raisins. "Try one of these little crab things. They're great!"

"You're paid to serve, oaf," Little Raisins snarled. "Not critique."

"Oh, I think you'll like these," the Tick said with a big grin on his face.

Arthur circled the room carrying another tray of food. As he passed between the Crease and Eyebrows Mulligan he saw the Tick stuffing a big handful of crab puffs down the throat of the Guy with Ears like Little Raisins. "Tick!" he yelled. "What are you doing?"

The Tick looked up and noticed that he was surrounded by a circle of angry-looking villains. He smiled at them. "Would . . . ah . . . anyone like a beverage?"

American Maid had moved over to Chippendale, hoping to grab the remote control from him. The Forehead was standing nearby. Suddenly he shouted, "Hey! I know who you are. You're American Maid!"

She clanged him on the forehead with her tray and then leapt across the room to join the Tick and Arthur, where they were about to battle a whole birthday party full of villains. There was a tense, silent moment until Chippendale started clapping his hands.

"Oh!" the Criminal Mastermind exclaimed. "Hors d'oeuvres *and* a floor show! How can I ever thank you?

Wait, I have an idea." He snapped his fingers. Chrome-dome pulled a lever in the wall.

Suddenly a trapdoor opened in the floor beneath the heroes. At the same time a steel cable dropped from the ceiling and lassoed the three into a tight bundle, suspending them over a pit.

The Tick flexed his mighty muscles. "Don't worry! I'll snap this steel cable like pasta!" As he strained to break the cable, it tightened around Arthur and American Maid.

"Uh . . . Tick?" Arthur managed to groan. "You're crushing us."

"Oh. Sorry."

Chippendale looked up at the tied heroes. "Another birthday present to me. Superheroes! This must be the part where I reveal my sinister plot to you and then you say—"

"You'll never get away with it, Chippendale!" American Maid yelled.

"Wait, wait," Chippendale said. "First comes my part." Chippendale pointed to a large window in the roof of the chamber. The full moon filled the window. Then he pulled a large cloth off a huge object. It looked like a big observatory telescope with a flashlight stuck into the back end. "Fellow villains! With my brand-new birthday toy—the awesome Geismann Heat Ray—I will make the ultimate graffiti statement. I will write my name across the face of the moon!"

Before American Maid could say her line again, the Tick exclaimed, "You'll never get away with it!"

Chippendale turned back to the heroes. "Unfortunately, you three won't be here for the historic signature. Because I'm going to feed you to my pit of ferocious, man-eating alligators . . . and cows!"

From deep in the dark pit came splashing, as if ghastly things were thrashing in the dank, filthy water below. As the three heroes hung in the air, they could hear the sinister hissing of alligators and the sinister mooing of cows.

Chippendale snapped his fingers again. The cable began lowering the heroes into the blackness of the horrible pit.

"You entered my house as caterers." Chippendale gloated with an evil laugh. "But you will *leave* it as *hors d'oeuvres!*"

4

Save Our Moon!

The Tick, Arthur, and American Maid were lowered slowly into the pit. They heard hissing and mooing and splashing below them.

The Tick said, "You fellows take the cows! I'll take the alligators!"

The three heroes came to rest at the bottom of the pit. They were standing in a foot of water. As their eyes became accustomed to the dimness, they could see ten man-eating alligators lying in the water. The alligators' stomachs were huge, as if they had recently eaten something very large. There was only one man-eating cow in the pit. She stood over in one corner, staring at the heroes, swishing her tail.

"Hey, look," the Tick yelled. "These alligators have all glutted themselves on cows!"

American Maid said, "Well, if they're full of cows, at least they won't be eating *us* anytime soon."

The steel cable loosened around the three heroes. The

Tick snapped it easily. American Maid stretched and said, "Now let's find a way out of here and stop that lunatic!" She and the Tick walked off into the darkness to search for an exit.

Arthur turned and looked at the last remaining cow. It was eyeing him. An alligator crawled toward the cow with its jaws wide open, hissing. The cow mooed. There was a tremendous chomping sound. Arthur's eyes widened and his jaw dropped. The cow stood there quietly, her stomach bulging—with an alligator. Arthur began backing away from the cow very slowly.

American Maid tapped the metal-lined wall of the pit. "I don't think this pit was built to get out of."

"Not a problem." The Tick smashed his powerful fist into the wall, knocking out a section of steel plating. Through the hole they could see the night sky. American Maid was impressed.

Outside the hole was a narrow ledge that ran along the cliff face. A thousand feet below was the river. The Tick and American Maid inched out onto the ledge. They pressed their backs against the rocks. The wind blew through his antennae and her hair.

Arthur followed them, but he didn't want to. He clutched the rocks until his knuckles were white. "You guys are crazy!"

The man-eating cow stuck her head out of the hole and stared at Arthur. Arthur inched farther away from her. The cow looked down. There was a clatter of hooves as she leapt out into the air and plummeted down with a triumphant moo. She splashed into the river, swam to the shore, and trotted away.

The heroes followed the treacherous path up until they were back at Chippendale's fortress. They climbed up the wall and soon they could look down through the window into the large room where the party continued. They could see the massive barrel of the Geismann Heat Ray cannon pointed at the moon.

Chippendale addressed the assembled bad guys. "I haven't always had friends like you. Because . . . because I was born different!" Several of the uglier criminals nodded with understanding. The light reflected off the deep, rich wood veneer of Chippendale's head as he continued, "Society shunned me. All my life, the world has tried to forget my face! But after tonight, they will never forget my name!" He stepped to the controls of the heat ray and peered through an aiming sight. "Professor Chromedome! Prepare to fire!"

The Tick whispered to his friends, "You know, I've been thinking. Is it against the law to write on the moon?"

Arthur said, "It doesn't matter if it's against the law, Tick. It's *wrong*! The moon has been precious to humankind since the dawn of civilization. Why, in earliest cultures, the moon was worshiped under many names: Hecate, Diana, Astarte. And the first farmers timed the sowing and reaping of their crops by the phases of the ancient moon." Arthur was impassioned. "Lovers, poets, philosophers, and dreamers have always looked to the moon for inspiration. Think of all that will be lost if Chairface succeeds!"

The Tick was caught up in the moment. "Yeah! And not only that, but what if defacing the moon could screw up the tides somehow . . . maybe even cause tidal waves?

And what if it makes everybody go crazy and engage in antisocial behavior and drive badly! And what if—"

"Tick! Tick!" Arthur shook his friend to snap his attention back to the real world. "Let's just say it would be bad, okay?"

Chippendale shouted, "Give me a C!"

All the criminals yelled "C!" as the heat ray shot up into the night. The beam hit the surface of the moon and cut a gigantic letter C across the lunar landscape. The party guests applauded wildly as Chippendale shouted, "Give me an H!"

As the heat ray began cutting the second letter into the moon, the Tick and American Maid argued about what to do. The Tick said, "But your plan didn't work! Let's use my plan now: brute force!"

"No way," she responded. "There're too many of them! We need a diversion."

"We don't have time for this," Arthur said quietly as he climbed into the window. "We've got to save the moon."

All the criminals were so excited by the heat ray demonstration that they didn't even notice Arthur as he walked through the room. When the beam was finished carving the letter *H* on the moon, Arthur reached up to the back of the cannon and took the flashlight that powered the heat ray. He turned and started sneaking away through the crowd of felons.

Chippendale called out again, "Now give me an A!"

There was no heat ray in response to Chairface's shout. Professor Chromedome pushed several buttons in panic. Then he looked at the empty hole in the rear of the cannon where the flashlight used to be. "I said give me an A!" Chippendale yelled louder.

Arthur tiptoed away from the criminals. Suddenly he had the uncomfortable feeling that he was being watched. He turned around slowly. Every single criminal in the room was staring at him. And they were really mad.

"Well, well, well. . . ," said Chippendale.

Arthur cleared his throat. Quietly he said, "Help."

The Tick's antennae pricked up. "That's Arthur!" he shouted. He and American Maid leapt through the window into the room.

The mob of villains was about to grab Arthur when the Tick and American Maid crashed into them. Ugly criminals went flying in all directions. The Tick grabbed the Crease and the Guy with Ears like Little Raisins. He shook them vigorously and tossed them across the room. Then he turned and grabbed the Deadly Nose by his lapels. The Deadly Nose reared back his head, and it made a sound like a gun cocking. Then he fired his nose at the Tick like a shotgun. The bullets bounced off the Tick's chest harmlessly.

The Tick glared down at the Deadly Nose. "Don't you blow your nose at *me,* mister!" Suddenly the Tick was tackled from behind by Jack Tuber, the potato-headed man of a thousand faces.

Meanwhile, American Maid chased Chairface Chippendale across the cavernous room. "You're not getting away *that* easily, Chairface!"

Chippendale raced to a wall where two swords were hanging over a shield. He tore one of the blades from its scabbard and held the cutlass toward American Maid. She stopped short and looked around. Then she seized a wooden chair and held it up in front of her, ready for battle.

"En garde!" she shouted at Chippendale. They began to duel, sword against chair. She skillfully deflected his blows, pressing him back against the wall. Then she smashed the chair over Chippendale's head. "Chairface, I'd like you to meet a long-lost cousin."

Arthur was pushed against the heat ray weapon by the menacing Professor Chromedome. "You'ff ruined effry-think," Chromedome complained. "You terrible rabbit perzon."

"I'm a terrible *moth* person!" Arthur said angrily. He took the flashlight he had stolen from the heat ray and shined it into Professor Chromedome's goggled eyes.

"Ach!" Chromedome screamed, throwing his arms up over his eyes. "I'm momentarily bline-ted!" Arthur shoved past Chromedome, knocking the mad professor off his feet.

Across the room, the Tick slammed Jack Tuber against the wall. The potato criminal's nose and eyes and ears popped off his head. Jack slumped to the ground.

The Tick smiled as he dusted off his hands and gave a heroic thumbs-up! Then he felt two leather-gloved hands clutch his throat. The hands belonged to the Butterfly Nutcase. And he tightened his viselike grip on the Tick's throat with a wrenching creak. The Nutcase had the strongest hands the Tick had ever felt, except for the time he had accidentally tried to strangle himself in his sleep. The Tick struggled in the ironlike fingers. He managed to reach up and, with a mighty effort, grab the sides of the Butterfly Nutcase's head and unscrew it. The hardware thug fell to the ground.

American Maid dueled Chippendale to a standstill. She held him at bay with her chair and cried, "The party's over, Chairface!"

"Guess again, Maid." Chippendale pressed a button on the wall. A panel slid back and he grabbed a ray gun before she could react.

Meanwhile, Arthur was searching for the Tick when suddenly he was cornered by the high-voltage Sheila Eel. She held out two electric eels. The slimy creatures crackled with deadly electricity and snapped their razor-sharp teeth at Arthur.

She smiled at the trembling sidekick. "Are you ready for a shocking experience?"

Arthur groped behind him with his hands along the table. "Please, no puns—I've had a very bad night." He grabbed a pitcher of water and threw it on the sparking Sheila Eel.

The electric villainess screamed as the wattage from her eel accessories arced through the water and past her stylish black rubber evening gown. She shook with pain. She smoked a little. And she fell down.

Arthur stared at her. Then the Tick reached over and grabbed him. "Quickly, chum! I need you!"

Chippendale had the drop on American Maid with a deadly ray gun. He aimed directly at her with a merciless chuckle. He tightened his finger on the trigger.

"Hold it right there, Chippendale!" the Tick shouted.

The Tick was balancing the huge heat ray cannon on his shoulder, pointing it at Chippendale. Arthur was hanging on to the back, holding the flashlight in the proper spot.

The Tick continued, "Surrender or I'm going to write this whole place off the face of the Earth!"

Chippendale dropped his ray gun. "Okay."

As the police stuffed Chippendale into the paddy wagon, he shouted, "You'll pay for this, all of you! No prison can hold Chairface Chippendale!"

Police Chief Louder, who always talked through a megaphone, said loudly to Chippendale, "Save it for the judge, buster!" Holding a half-eaten crab puff in his other hand, he turned to American Maid and the Tick. "Say, these little crab things are great!" Then he spoke on the record again. "You've done your City a great service!"

"We're proud to serve, sir!" the Tick yelled back. "Good night!"

As the police van drove away, American Maid patted the Tick on the back and said, "Well, I have to admit I was worried, but you guys are pretty good superheroes. Maybe we'll work together again."

The Tick smiled as she climbed into her catering van. "Yes! It was good saving the moon with you, American Maid! Drive carefully now." The van roared away, the fiberglass croissant on top glowing in the darkness.

The Tick said, "A heart of gold beats beneath that big fiberglass croissant, Arthur. And thank goodness for it. It's spirit like hers that allowed us to thwart Chairface's evil scheme. And thwart we did!"

"I—I guess so." Arthur looked up. He could see the letters *C* and *H* scratched across the face of the moon.

Off in the distance, there was a low moo. Then the man-eating cow walked away into the darkness.

Part 4

THE TICK
VS.
DINOSAUR NEIL

1

A Day of Science

The alarm clock buzzed at 6:30 A.M., waking Arthur from a sound sleep. He stumbled out of bed and shuffled into the kitchen to make coffee.

"Mmm . . . patrol. Morning patrol. . . ," he muttered to himself.

The Tick strolled into the kitchen, wide awake and cheerful. "Good morning, Arthur! And a fine morning it is!"

"I'm up, I'm up," Arthur said sleepily. "Morning patrol . . . I got it."

"*No!*" the Tick said. Then he began rummaging through the junk drawer. The Tick reached for something in the bottom of the drawer with a little too much power, and his hand crashed through the wood. "No patrols today, little friend. Today is our day off. We're going to spend quality time together!" The Tick shoved a brightly colored brochure in Arthur's face. The brochure had pictures of strange animal skeletons. "We're going to Dinosaur Gulch!"

An hour later, the Tick and Arthur sat in the backseat of the bus heading for Dinosaur Gulch. The Tick read the brochure out loud. "Guided tours daily of a working dinosaur dig. Come watch our team of expert scientists dig up real dinosaur bones." The Tick punched Arthur lightly on the arm. "Dinosaur bones, sleepy sidekick! Fun and educational!"

Arthur covered his mouth as he yawned. "Whatever. As long as we're back by six and Dot isn't kept waiting."

The Tick smiled. "Ah, yes, Dot. The sister." He had met Dot before and was fond of her.

Arthur said, "That's right. She still doesn't approve of my superhero lifestyle. I only asked her to dinner to show that I'm still a sane and loving person."

The Tick said in a booming voice, "Family values! You're crazy for that sibling!"

"Yeah," Arthur said. "So tonight, can you just . . . tone it down?"

The Tick answered, "Not a problem, gentle avenger. I will suppress my every urge!"

Arthur rolled his eyes.

Dinosaur Gulch was very exciting. The sign was exciting enough for most people. Two giant tyrannosaur skeletons stood on the sides of the entrance holding a sign in their menacing jaws that read WELCOME TO DINOSAUR GULCH. The gulch was a deep, winding canyon with sheer bedrock walls. Fossil dinosaur skeletons were embedded in the cliff faces. Bones were scattered along the floor of the canyon. Tents and equipment dotted the area.

Tourists wandered around in groups, asking questions of the scientists who worked there. The visitors were led around the site by the chief scientist, known as Dinosaur Neil. Dinosaur Neil was dressed in a rubber dinosaur suit, looking like a tyrannosaur. He pointed out interesting facts about the different skeletons that were being unearthed in the area.

"And that concludes this afternoon's tour," Dinosaur Neil said as he led a group of tourists out of Dinosaur Gulch. "As chief paleontologist at the gulch, I'd like to thank you for coming and remind you that we have T-shirts and other souvenirs here in the Gift Shoppe." Neil saw the Tick and Arthur looking at the gifts.

"I must say," Neil said to them. "It's a pleasure to see superheroes taking such an interest in science."

The Tick shook Neil's hand. "Wonderful tour, Dinosaur Neil! I never knew I could learn so much. Now, just to retain it!"

Just then Buffy, one of Dinosaur Neil's assistants, rushed in carrying a large bone. "Dinosaur Neil! Look!" she cried, handing him the bone. "We found a *femur*!"

Neil took the bone and inspected it. "Hmmm. Apatosaurus. Beautifully preserved." Then he thought to himself, "Just what I need." He looked at the Tick and Arthur again. "You boys like science? Why not come back to my tent. I'll show you the kind of science you can't find in a textbook."

The Tick and Arthur followed Dinosaur Neil back through the gulch to a large laboratory tent. Inside the tent was a strange machine. Neil placed the bone on a whirring conveyor belt and it entered the machine. A laser beam scanned it. Lights glowed and blinked. There was a glass cylinder attached to the machine by hoses. Inside the glass cylinder a thick liquid bubbled loudly. A computer screen began to flash combinations of the letters *A, T, C,* and *G,* the symbols for the chemical elements of DNA. The Tick stared in awe at the machine.

Dinosaur Neil picked up a glass lab dish labeled PASTA SALAD and began to eat. Behind him hung a big sign that read DO NOT EAT IN LAB.

"You see," Neil said between mouthfuls. "I believe I can grow a dinosaur with the help of these fossils."

Arthur stroked his chin and said, "I don't know. That doesn't sound possible."

Neil yelled back, "It is! I saw it in a movie once! My machine synthesizes living tissue from fossilized DNA patterns."

"Hey, smooth!" The Tick was impressed.

Neil set down his dish of pasta salad next to another dish full of lumpy mush labeled DINOSAUR TISSUE. He picked up the tissue dish. "Look here, I've already grown some dinosaur tissue." He gestured with his fork, which he still held in his right hand. "I have to keep it in a solution of acetylsalicylic acid. Otherwise I'm afraid it would just keep on growing."

Neil took a forkful from the dish and put it in his mouth. While chewing he said, "I figure I'll have a fully functional dinosaur by the middle of next month." He swallowed. Then his eyes grew wide with fear and he gasped. He had eaten a forkful of *dinosaur* tissue!

The Tick said, "Bad move, Neil."

Dinosaur Neil clutched his throat and held his breath. He gagged for a second. Then he let out his breath and shrugged. "Oh, well, no harm done."

Dinosaur Neil led the two heroes out to the Gift Shoppe, where the Tick bought a T-shirt that read I DIG DINOSAUR NEIL. "Too bad you boys have to leave so soon," Dinosaur Neil said. "If you could stick around, you could catch the fireworks and the Parade of Extinction."

The Tick perked up. "Fireworks? Extinction? Keen!"

Arthur tugged on the Tick's elbow. He cleared his throat. "Uh . . . Tick? Remember *Dot*?"

The Tick waved at Dinosaur Neil as Arthur pulled him toward the bus stop.

That evening in Dinosaur Neil's tent there were strange noises—metal rattling and small plastic bottles falling to the ground. Inside the tent everything was a mess, as if a beast had rampaged through. The first-aid box had been knocked off the tent pole. Plastic medicine bottles and rolls of gauze bandages were scattered around. The scientists in the gulch heard odd roars almost like those of a dinosaur.

Inside the tent, green scaly hands struggled to open a little aspirin bottle. They looked like Dinosaur Neil's hands, only larger. Neil's voice, choked with pain, said, "Hands getting bigger . . . brain getting smaller. Child-proof cap . . . impossible!" Then there was a huge roar of dinosaur rage, louder than the last one, followed by the stomping sound of monstrous footsteps. Lying on the floor of the tent in the darkness was the Dinosaur Neil rubber costume. It was in shreds, burst apart at the seams.

2

Monsters on the Rampage and Dinner with Dot

"That's the timer!" Arthur shouted. "The fettuccine's ready! The sauce is done!" He raced around the kitchen, trying to finish dinner before his sister Dot arrived. The Tick, still wearing his wonderful Dinosaur Neil T-shirt, tossed the salad. Arthur handed him two cloves of garlic. "Here, crush these."

The Tick took a clove in each mighty hand and tightened his grip until the strong aroma of garlic attacked his supernostrils. He recoiled and said, "Oh, the stink of it!"

Arthur finished setting the table, which had been dragged into the living room, when the doorbell rang. "She's here!" he cried. "Tick, take off that shirt!"

The Tick removed his T-shirt as Arthur unlocked several dead bolts on the door and opened it. Dot was about Arthur's size, but slimmer, with brown hair cut in a bob. She wore a plaid skirt and glasses. She was carrying a cake box.

"Dot! Hi!" Arthur said. The Tick grinned behind him. Arthur let her into the apartment and closed the door. "You remember the Tick, don't you?"

"Yes," Dot said. "I remember the Tick."

The Tick said, "Oh, Dot, you look lovely tonight. Your hair is like a halo of mouse-brown fire! Whatever did you do with it?"

"I washed it," she answered flatly.

Dinosaur Gulch was closed. The lights were off and the grounds were dark. Buffy was walking to her car in the parking lot when she heard rustling and chomping noises from high in a nearby tree. She turned to look and saw a twenty-foot-tall dinosaur emerge from the shadows, his mouth full of branches and leaves.

"Dinosaur Neil?" she asked. The dinosaur looked down at her. "Are you okay? You look a little . . . big."

Dinosaur Neil turned from her and stomped off, away from the gulch. He let out a deafening roar. Buffy decided it might be wise to call the police.

"Well, Arthur," Dot said, taking a bite of pasta, "this is delicious. I'm glad to see you still have time to cook."

Arthur nodded. "Thanks. The Tick tossed the salad."

"Yes!" the Tick said. "Quite a challenge!" The Tick used his fork to wind his whole plate of fettuccine into a big ball and popped it into his mouth. He smiled with satisfaction, one noodle trailing out of his mouth.

The television was playing in the background. A news alert broke into the broadcast of *The Mummy Speaks*. Sally Vacuum, the Channel 17 reporter, said, "The authorities have issued a Citywide alert: Dinosaur Neil, head paleontologist and tour guide at Dinosaur Gulch, is now seventy feet tall and walking down Main Street." A camera showed Dinosaur Neil, bigger than before, lumbering through the streets of the City. Cars were skidding to avoid him. People were running in panic.

"Dinosaur Neil is still growing," Sally Vacuum continued. "And no one knows where it will end." The camera pulled back to show that the mysterious superhero Die Fledermaus was standing next to Sally on the street where she was reporting the story. "We have with us one of the City's superheroes, Die Fledermaus." As the dark hero tried to find the most heroic pose for television, Dinosaur Neil could be seen far in the background. He turned and headed toward the camera.

"Die Fledermaus," Sally asked, "can you tell us what the superhero community plans to do about this menace?" Citizens were running for their lives. Dinosaur Neil stomped closer and closer.

Die Fledermaus responded in his deep, scary voice. "Good question, Sally. Actually, I think we'll just sit it out and wait for the National Guard."

Dinosaur Neil was barely twenty feet behind the newswoman and the hero. His green feet were the size of station wagons. The camera shook every time he took a step.

"This has been Sally Vacuum at the scene of the Dinosaur Neil crisis," said the reporter, signing off.

"So," Die Fledermaus asked Sally quietly, "when's this going to be on?"

Back in the apartment, chocolate cake was being served. The Tick could barely stay in his seat. He was anxious to get involved in the Dinosaur Neil crisis. Arthur warned him quietly, "Tick! Tone it down." The Tick sat perfectly still, gritting his teeth, his face turning red with effort. Arthur turned to Dot. "This cake is delicious. What is it?"

Dot said, "Chocolate."

The City police had surrounded Dinosaur Neil. Bright spotlights arced across the night sky, lighting up the rampaging Dinosaur Neil. Police Chief Louder stood next to a spotlight that played across the giant beast. He shouted up with a megaphone, "Dinosaur Neil! Please exit the City! We have a team of expert scientists to give you assistance . . . and a pair of pants!" In response, Dinosaur Neil smashed a nearby movie theater that was playing *Gorgonzola vs. Mothzilla.*

At that moment, Mayor Blank sat in his office talking on the phone. An aide stood at the window watching as Dinosaur Neil lumbered through the distant streets, lit by spotlights. The mighty roars of the reptile echoed through the City.

"Well," Mayor Blank said, "I wouldn't say he's rampaging per se." He covered the phone and spoke to his assistant. "The National Guard says it won't come unless a dinosaur is *officially rampaging.*"

The assistant pointed at Dinosaur Neil just as the great beast smashed a water tower off a building. The water roared into the streets.

The mayor spoke into the phone. "I think we can confirm that rampage."

Back at the apartment, the sound of forks clinking on

plates was drowned out by the thunderous footfalls of Dinosaur Neil. The heroes tried very hard not to listen to it. Then Dinosaur Neil could be seen outside the window. Arthur turned around to see Neil stomp by. "I'm sorry, Dot," he said.

"Arthur. . . ," Dot warned.

Arthur ignored his sister and turned to his partner. "Tick, let's go."

The Tick jumped from his chair, every muscle bursting with superhero energy. "Now you're talking, chum. To action!"

The Tick and Arthur raced out the front door of the apartment and down the hall. Dot sat at the table, calling after them, "Don't expect me to do the dishes!"

3

A Prescription for Danger!

"We've got to cut him off!" the Tick said as he and Arthur ran up the stairs onto the roof. Dinosaur Neil was passing by their building. "Maybe I can talk some sense into him." The Tick ran to the edge of the roof and shouted, "Hey, Dinosaur Neil! Whatcha doing?"

Dinosaur Neil stared down at the Tick without recognition. He roared and slammed a giant reptilian-clawed hand onto the Tick, crunching the hero into the roof. The Tick got to his feet as the monster lurched away and he called out, "You're rubbing me the wrong way, friend!"

The Tick followed Dinosaur Neil down the street, leaping from rooftop to rooftop. Arthur fluttered after him. The Tick took a powerful jump and landed on Neil's leathery skin. Expecting that his colossal strength would overpower the dinosaur, the Tick began trying to knock Neil off his clawed feet. But Neil paid no attention to the epic struggle taking place on his shoulder.

Arthur flew very hard to keep up. "Wait! Wait! Tick, I have an idea!"

The Tick continued to grunt with exertion, trying to wrestle the great beast to the ground. Neil finally noticed the annoying superhero. The dinosaur lifted his hand and flicked the Tick like a bug. The Tick went flying, crashing into the ground and skidding backward. He tore a long trench in the street until he finally came to a stop.

Arthur landed next to the mound of dirt at the end of the trench and looked into the hole. "I think I've got an idea," he repeated.

The Tick sat up in the trench. He stared straight ahead. "Well, mine didn't work. What's yours?"

"This morning Neil said that he had to keep his dinosaur tissue in a solution of acetylsalicylic acid to keep it from growing!"

The Tick stood up. He was still a little confused from the blow. "What?"

Arthur said, "Acetylsalicyclic acid is aspirin! If we can give Neil a dinosaur-sized dose of aspirin, he might shrink back to normal!"

"I'll try anything once," the Tick said.

Inside Bang Pharmaceuticals Drugstore, the Tick hummed along to the Muzak playing over the store's speakers while Arthur talked to the kindly pharmacist.

"Let's see," the pharmacist said. "We usually recommend two aspirins for an average-sized adult. Now, how much did you say your friend weighs?"

Arthur thought for a second. "About a hundred and eighty tons."

"Oh." The pharmacist nodded, then turned and walked to the back of the pharmacy. "Okay, give me a minute."

The Tick tapped his foot to the music and asked, "Do you think Dot is mad at you?"

"Maybe." Arthur sighed. "But she has to understand that this is what I want to do with my life."

Meanwhile, the Human Bullet was having a barbecue with his wife and son in their backyard. They ate hot dogs as they watched bugs hit the bug zapper. Suddenly, three National Guard helicopters roared overhead, flying toward the City. The Human Bullet threw down his hot dog with a look of determination. He stood up. "The National Guard! Hmmm . . . this could mean the City needs the Human Bullet!"

He rushed off in the direction of the big cannon he kept in the backyard. His son picked up his lemonade and followed. Mrs. Human Bullet frowned and took another bite of her hot dog. The Human Bullet climbed into the cannon as his son took his position by the button. "Fire me, boy!" the Human Bullet said. The cannon boomed and the Human Bullet flew away to do battle with evil.

Dinosaur Neil had paused in his reptilian rampage in the parking lot of the City Mall. There he was surrounded by the tanks and cannons of the National Guard. The National Guard commander wondered why a monster had to show up on the one weekend a month he spent with the Guard. He checked to see if his tanks were in position to open fire on Dinosaur Neil. Spotlights shone on Neil's green hide. The commander raised his arm. "Prepare to fire!"

"Wait! Sir! Wait! Don't shoot!" Arthur shouted. He and the Tick ran up to the National Guard commander. The Tick had a four-and-a-half-foot-long aspirin tablet strapped to his back. Arthur said, "We can save him! All we need is five minutes."

The commander eyed them. "What can you do in five minutes, civilians?"

"*Superheroes,* sir," Arthur corrected him. "We're going to give him an aspirin."

The Tick saluted and hurried off toward Dinosaur Neil.

"Hey!" the commander shouted, trying to stop him.

Arthur stepped in front of the commander. "You may not know this, sir, but nearly two thousand years ago a brew made from white willow leaves was recommended for gout." The commander stared at him. Arthur continued: "Today, a remedy based on that same chemical— aspirin!—is the most widely used medicine in the world." The commander tried to seem interested, but he was a little busy. After all, there was a raging reptilian beast destroying the City. Still Arthur went on. "But aspirin is strong medicine, and should be taken only as directed. And children should never—*ever*—take aspirin except under the supervision of their parents or a licensed physician."

Even while distracted, the commander recognized sound and rational thinking. He said, "That's good advice."

The Tick skidded to a stop not far from one of Dinosaur Neil's huge, scaly feet. "Hey, Arthur! How are we going to get Neil to take this pill?"

Dinosaur Neil heard the Tick's voice and looked down.

Arthur shouted, "Tick! Look out!"

"What?"

Suddenly, Dinosaur Neil lowered his head and his fearsome jaws closed over the Tick!

4

Take That Thing Out of Your Mouth

Dinosaur Neil calmly lifted his head with the Tick trapped inside his mouth.

"Hey!" shouted the Tick in surprise.

Arthur screamed, "Tick!"

The commander raised his eyebrows. "Looks like your friend's being devoured." He turned back to his troops. "Okay, everybody . . . ready . . . aim—"

"No!" Arthur shouted. "Give the Tick a chance! He's nigh invulnerable. He'll be okay." Then Arthur quietly said to himself, "He's got to be."

Dinosaur Neil was having trouble chewing the mighty mouthful. Inside the giant jaws, the Tick fell onto the massive molar teeth and Neil crunched down on him. The Tick grunted, reached up, and pried Neil's jaw open. Then he rolled off the teeth and onto Neil's gigantic, wet tongue. He slid down the tongue into the back of Neil's throat. Just before he went down the dinosaur's hatch, the

Tick made a stupendous leap and grabbed hold of Neil's uvula, that little thing that hangs down in the back of everyone's throat. He looked down into the black, cavernous maw that was Neil's gut.

The Tick unstrapped the giant aspirin tablet from his back. "Down the hatch, big boy." He hurled the four-and-a-half-foot pill down into the darkness of the stomach.

Just at that second, the Human Bullet flew into the picture. With a high-pitched wail, he smashed into Dinosaur Neil's stomach and then fell to the ground. Dinosaur Neil grunted with the impact and coughed.

Inside the mouth, the Tick clutched the uvula, riding out the massive cough. Then the aspirin tablet popped back up and out of Neil's throat. It smacked the Tick in the back of the head. He rubbed his head and gasped in alarm as he saw the pill slide to the front of the monstrous mouth, where it came to rest under the tip of Neil's tongue. It could fall out at any moment. The Tick swung back and forth on the uvula and somersaulted up to the front of Neil's mouth. He landed on the tongue and grabbed it in his best wrestling hold. The tongue smashed him against the hard, white wall of teeth. The Tick rode the powerful tongue all around the mouth, never releasing it from his superhammerlock. Then it pressed him tightly up against the roof of Neil's mouth.

"Tongue-tied," the Tick groaned. He could see the aspirin tablet on the floor of Neil's mouth, but it was out of reach. He tightened his grip on the tongue, squeezing it with every ounce of his supermagnificent strength. The tongue struggled briefly, but then succumbed to the superior might of the Tick. The tongue fell to the floor of the mouth.

The Tick grabbed the aspirin like a football and hurled it back down the cavelike throat. "Aspirin away!" he called. Far below he could hear a splash as the pill landed in Dinosaur Neil's stomach and Neil gave a big gulp.

Back outside, Arthur and the National Guard commander saw the dinosaur swallow. "Well," the commander said, "I guess that's it for the blue guy. But he went down fighting."

Arthur had tears in his goggles. "It—it can't be!"

Suddenly, two blue hands appeared between Neil's teeth. The Tick began to force Neil's jaws apart. The dinosaur couldn't resist the power of the Tick, who soon stood triumphant on Neil's lower teeth. The National Guardsmen cheered. Arthur smiled too. The Tick leapt to the ground.

"Tick!" Arthur cried. "You're okay!" He hugged his mighty friend. Then he looked down in disgust. Now he was covered with dinosaur spit too.

The Tick turned to see that Neil was back to his normal size and species. He was no longer a dinosaur. Unfortunately for Neil, he was also naked. Luckily, he was standing behind a big tank. He smiled and waved at the cheering National Guardsmen.

Several nights later in Arthur's apartment, the Tick and Arthur were entertaining Dot again. This time their guest was not just Dot, because Dinosaur Neil was with them. He was in his rubber dinosaur suit again, but he was polite enough not to wear the head at the table.

"So, tell me, Tick," Dinosaur Neil said. "When you were fighting my tongue, was that weird for you or anything?"

"Unique, Neil," the Tick answered. "But all in a day's work for a superhero."

Dinosaur Neil smiled. "Well, you saved my life."

The Tick shrugged and gestured toward Arthur. "Don't thank me. Thank Arthur. The aspirin was his idea." Arthur looked down modestly.

Dot leaned over and touched Arthur's hand. "Well, Arthur, I have to admit it. You guys saved Dinosaur Neil and the whole City. But it's still your turn to do the dishes."

Music played in the living room as Dot and Dinosaur Neil danced. Water ran in the kitchen as the Tick and Arthur washed dishes.

The Tick wore rubber gloves and was sponging a plate, lost in thought. Warm, soapy water did that to him.

"Once again, my friend," he said to Arthur, "we find that science is a two-headed beast." He handed the plate to Arthur, who began drying. "One head is nice—it gives us aspirin and other modern conveniences." The Tick splashed vigorously in the water. "But the other head is bad! Oh, beware the other head of science, Arthur! It bites! And it can really ruin a good day off!"

Part 5

THE TICK
VS.
EL SEED

1

When Good Shrubs Go Bad

It began on a beautiful day in the City. The sun rose. The birds sang. The flowers stretched their petals—and cried out in rebellion! It was the day of the worst plant uprising in the history of the City. Perhaps the worst one in the history of humankind! Although the Irish potato famine was pretty bad—but that's another story.

The elderly Mrs. Brushbottom opened her window the way she did every morning to greet her carnations. They grew in a flower box outside her window and she loved them.

"Good morning, little flower faces," she said. "Did we all make a lot of oxygen last night?" As she leaned over to smell them, one carnation drew back and smacked her on the nose. *Phup!* Mrs. Brushbottom was startled. Then the flower struck her again. "What's gotten into you?" Mrs. Brushbottom asked. The flowers didn't answer her. They reached out with their stems and leaves. They entangled Mrs. Brushbottom and yanked her out the window.

Across town, Sid Stern was delivering trees to a house in the suburbs. His green truck—with the sign SID 'N' AL: THE PINE BARONS—was parked in the driveway. In the back of the truck were six saplings that Sid had come to plant. As he was talking with the owner of the house, the trees began to shiver and move. Suddenly two trees leapt from the truckbed and shuffled up to the doors of the truck. The trees jumped in and started the engine. Before Sid could say anything, they drove the truck away. The saplings in the back yelled "Wheeee!" in delight as the wind blew through their branches.

"Hey!" shouted Sid. But it was too late.

At the City Golf Course, Ted and Marty were enjoying a round of golf. Ted lined up his tee shot.

"So you're telling me," Ted said as he wiggled into his stance, "there's *bad* cholesterol and *good* cholesterol?" Ted swung and his ball sailed away.

"Right, right," said Marty, watching Ted's shot. The ball flew into a stand of trees to the right of the fairway. "Ohh! In the rough!"

After Marty hit his shot, they strolled through the green grass. Ted struggled into the woods to look for his ball. He hacked at the dense shrubbery with a sand wedge. Finally he spotted his little white ball under a bush.

"Found it!" Ted shouted. But he didn't see the mob of shrubs that had surrounded him. They closed in angrily. Ted looked up and saw the plants moving toward him.

"Marty?" he called out. Then the vicious vegetation rushed at him, knocking him to the ground. "Marty!" he shouted.

Ted and Marty would not finish their round of golf that day.

Meanwhile, at Angry Hank's Fat Pig Texas Bar-B-Q, the Tick and Arthur had been enjoying the Eat Till You Fall Over chili lunch. Suddenly, a cactus that had been standing politely in the corner ever since the restaurant opened started making trouble. It ran around sticking customers with its thorns. The shouts of pain caused the Tick to look up from his chili. He saw three more cacti pull themselves loose from their pots and poke customers. Arthur wiped the steam from his goggles with alarm—his goggles always steamed up when he ate chili.

When a rowdy cactus tried to poke the Tick, he jumped up and grabbed it and tossed it across the room. It crashed over the bar and bounced onto the floor. Then the Tick and Arthur stood back as the cactus got up, wiped itself off, and joined with its three allies for another attack.

"Careful, chum," the Tick said to Arthur. They backed up as the cacti approached. "I don't like the look of these prickly succulents!"

Arthur was holding a pair of bull horns, which he had taken off the wall of Angry Hank's, out in front of him for protection. "What's happening to the plants in the City?"

"They do seem restless," the Tick agreed. He backed hard into a wall and more of Angry Hank's quaint decorations fell off. In this case a big cowboy hat landed on the Tick's head and a lasso of rope dropped into his hand. The

Tick smiled like a buckaroo. "Hmmm . . . just like the movies."

"Aha!" the Tick yelled as he threw his lariat. It looped over the four cacti. He pulled the rope tight. The cacti were pressed against each other's spines and began to cry, "Ow! Ow! Ow! Ow!" The Tick tripped the bad plants like an expert calf bulldogger and hog-tied them, chanting, "Over . . . under . . . into a loop . . . then the rabbit goes into the hole." The knot grew bigger and bigger, but the Tick kept tying. "Then this little piggy went to market . . . then . . . Kentucky secedes from the Union . . ." He stood up. "There!"

He yanked the thorny troublemakers up to his eye level and stared at them sternly. "Okay, cacti! What are you up to? What's going on? Give me the skinny."

"Ow! Ow! Ow! Ow!" the cacti said.

Arthur said, "Tick, they're plants. They can't really talk. Besides, it's not just them. This is happening all over the City. Something else must be behind this. Something . . . weird."

West of the City was a belt of fertile farmland. In the middle of this idyllic setting, next to a vast cornfield, rested an old, run-down Victorian farmhouse. Behind the farmhouse was a strangely modern greenhouse. And inside the greenhouse was a strange figure. It was El Seed!

El Seed was a plant who walked like a person. He had a head like a daisy, but with bright yellow pointed petals. His arms and legs were leaves and stalks. He wore the strikingly attractive lime-green suit of a bullfighter. And he was a criminal genius!

El Seed had a laboratory in the greenhouse. There were test tubes, glass beakers, and Bunsen burners everywhere. Strange chemicals bubbled while the Bee Twins, El Seed's most trusted assistants, buzzed from tube to tube fixing and adjusting.

"Bee Twins!" El Seed called in his accented voice.

"Yes, El Seed?"

"You know what I hate?"

"You hate humans," the Bee Twins answered, because they did know what El Seed hated.

"I hate humans," El Seed said anyway. "They really get my goat. I'm not so fond of goats either! In fact, the whole animal kingdom really fries my fronds!" El Seed watched eagerly as a bright green liquid dripped into a beaker. "When the Earth was young the plant kingdom was in the driver's seat. Oh, there was the occasional animal. The bees, for example, flitting from flower to flower . . . not for conquest—but for love!" The green liquid then ran from the beaker through a tube into a large glass tank where it mixed with a clear liquid. This mixture started bubbling. El Seed yelled in anger, "These animals, they are the troublemakers! Always moving around with their feet and their wings and their wheels!

"They wear us! They eat us!" El Seed continued his speech. The mixture in the tank stopped bubbling, so he opened a valve and the green solution dripped into a small glass vial. "They put us in pots! They squeeze us for juice! It's grotesque. But soon all this will change." He held up the vial of green liquid. "This Vegetation Vitalizer will free all plant life to rise up against the animal oppressor!"

El Seed stalked outside the greenhouse. The Bee Twins

followed him. On the lawn there was a large object covered by a tarpaulin. "No longer must we vitalize one plant at a time! This time, we will get the whole City in a single whack!" He pulled back the tarp and revealed an old-fashioned, single-engine biplane. "I have rented a crop duster!"

As he basked in his glory, the stolen truck driven by the trees roared up the long drive from the highway. It screeched to a halt near the airplane. The trees yelled, "Yee-haa!"

El Seed smiled. "Ooh! Free truck!"

2

Don't Go in the Park Without a Whip and a Chair

Back in the City, the Tick and Arthur were high above the streets, leaping from building to building, on patrol for more vegetable uprisings.

"I don't get it, Arthur," the Tick puzzled between leaps. "I've always operated under the assumption that plants are good. And now this!" He stopped to think. "I just can't get my mind around it."

Arthur hovered nearby. Then he heard a strange buzzing sound. He looked up and saw a crop duster whip around the corner of a building and bear down on him. Arthur flapped wildly to get out of the way. The airplane zoomed past, nearly clipping Arthur's wings. He tumbled in the air.

The Tick stared at the plane. "That's a violation of your airspace! Follow that plane!"

From the cockpit of the plane, El Seed looked down at the passing rooftops. "Animals, your days are numbered!"

He was wearing goggles. He poured a drop of the bright green vitalizer from the glass vial into a funnel. The drop passed into a larger tank where it mixed with water and then through pipes out to spray nozzles on both wings. "One part vitalizer!" El Seed yelled. "To a million zillion parts water! The recipe for revolution!"

El Seed flew the airplane over the City Park, a pleasant rectangle of green in the midst of all the concrete and steel towers. He came in low over the treetops and released a spray of green mist. Then he climbed and began to wheel around for another pass.

The Tick landed on the edge of a rooftop overlooking the park. "Why would they dust the park? There are no crops!"

"Look!" Arthur shouted, pointing to the park. Trees— the charming maples, majestic oaks, and shady elms—were starting to wriggle and tear their roots out of the ground, stretching their branches all around. "Those trees are going nuts! We've got to stop that plane!"

The airplane sprayed a second misty green coat over the park. Then it began to climb again, right in the direction of the Tick and Arthur. The Tick waited until just the right moment, then he leapt out and grabbed hold of the plane's wheels as it passed by.

El Seed laughed with evil glee as he gained altitude. But suddenly a blue arm clutched the fuselage and the Tick's face popped up next to El Seed. They looked at each other for a second. And then they both screamed in surprise and shock. El Seed let go of the plane's flight stick and the crop duster began to spiral out of control toward the ground.

El Seed shouted, "Off my plane, blue monkey!"

"I don't know who you are or what you're up to, mister," the Tick said firmly, "but I want this plane on the ground pronto!"

"No!" El Seed responded. "I rented it for the whole day!"

The Tick lunged for the plane's controls. "Give me that stick, petal head!"

El Seed scuffled with the Tick. In the melee, he dropped the glass vial of green vitalizer. It flipped through the air and hit the Tick in the chest. The glass broke and the dark green liquid spilled all over the Tick. He lost his grip on the airplane, surprised by the tingly green stuff that washed over him. He fell back and plummeted to the ground.

El Seed regained control of the plane. As he flew away, he shouted, "And don't come back, animal!"

The Tick dropped to earth, trailing a cloud of green mist. He crashed through the trees and hit the ground, punching out a big crater. Since he was nigh invulnerable, he was unhurt by the fall. But the vitalizer was having a strange effect on him.

Arthur swooped down into the trees and hovered over the crater as the Tick shook his head. "Are you okay?" Arthur asked.

The Tick looked around curiously. "I feel funky." The trees were moving, branches and roots rustling and crackling. The two heroes were surrounded by angry elms and oaks. "Monkey . . . funky," the Tick said.

Arthur landed to help his friend. "Come on, Tick! Get with it! We've got to get out of here!" Arthur helped him past the trees that reached down and tried to grab them with their branches. Just as they were coming to a clearing, a tree snagged Arthur and lifted him thirty feet off the ground. "Tick!" Arthur shouted. "Help me! Get me down!"

The Tick punched the air a few times. He was hopelessley dopey. "Put that monkey down. . . ," he said to no one in particular.

Outside the front gate of the City Park, a beige sedan screeched to a halt. It was no ordinary sedan. It was the vehicle of the Civic-minded Five! They were the City's most thoughtful and involved group of superheroes. They even sponsored a Little League baseball team.

Feral Boy was driving the car. He was a hairy guy who slobbered and smelled like a dog that needed a bath. Sitting next to him was the leader of the group, Four-legged Man, who actually did have four legs. In the backseat were Jungle Janet, Captain Mucilage, who was trailing strings of glue, and the Carpeted Man.

"Hmmm," said Four-legged Man. "Looks like the park's gone bad. This could be a job for . . ."

Four of the five group members shouted, "The Civic-minded Five!" Feral Boy barked, "Arf! Arf! Arf! Arf!" They all climbed from the car and rushed into the park. Suddenly, Four-legged Man spotted several teenagers who were trapped high above the ground in the branches of angry trees.

He said, "Top priority—get those kids down! All right, Civic-minded Five . . ."

"Let's make a difference!" they all shouted as they ran for the roughneck trees, except for Feral Boy, who growled and snorted and barked.

3

The Tick Is Fertile

The Civic-minded Five leapt into action to save the teenagers from the trees. Captain Mucilage raised his hands and said, "I'll stop those trees with my streams of high-pressure mucilage!" He fired powerful glue from his hands into the trees. "Let's get sticky!"

"Yuck! Eueeew!" screamed the kids.

The Carpeted Man shuffled past Captain Mucilage down the main path. "By rubbing my carpeted feet over any surface," he said, "I can create a tremendous charge of static electricity!" A vicious shrub lunged at him, so he touched the bush and shocked it. "Gotcha!" But as the Carpeted Man continued to shuffle forward, he began to sweat. "I'm so hot in this suit!" He wobbled, then fainted from the heat.

Feral Boy climbed into the trees that held the teens captive. When he got closer, the kids began screaming in fear. They weren't afraid of the trees; they were afraid of Feral Boy.

"Don't worry, kids," Four-legged Man shouted. "He's had all his shots!"

Jungle Janet raced down the main path deeper into the park. "I'll use my awesome strength and jungle savvy to see if anyone is in trouble on the bike path!" She leapt up, grabbing on to the branches and swinging through the trees. She batted away grasping tree limbs that blocked her way. She was born to live in the jungle and she moved through the limbs with the strength of a great ape, the skill of a gibbon, and the agility of a ring-tailed lemur! She tore through leaves and smashed branches that tried to encircle her waist. She was in shape from years of jungle living.

Nearby, Arthur was still trapped. The trees were shaking him upside down. Quarters and dimes fell out of his pocket. "Cut it out!" he yelled. "Hey, my change! Somebody better help me!"

The Tick was delirious. "Monkey! Monkey . . ." He stumbled around on the ground. Then he felt something strange. He looked down and saw a red rose sprouting from his chest. It looked pretty against the blue background of his costume.

Jungle Janet paused on a branch, listening with ears as sensitive as a jaguar's. She heard Arthur's cries for help. And she recognized his voice; she had met him at a superhero brunch. She somersaulted over to him and wrenched him free of the trees' grasp. Once on the ground, she asked, "Are you okay? What are you doing here?"

The Tick staggered over to Janet. He picked the rose off his chest and handed it to her. "Janet. Flower?"

Arthur explained. "All I know is there's this guy in this airplane and he was spraying the park and everything went crazy and the Tick jumped up on his airplane and they had this big fight and the Tick fell off the airplane and he was all glowing and green and now he's like this!"

The Tick plucked a potato that had suddenly grown under his arm. "Potato," he said.

Moments later, everyone was back outside the main gate. The Civil-minded Five had rescued the teenagers and Jungle Janet helped Arthur get the Tick to safety. The Tick had several little maple trees growing on him. Janet had the Tick's rose stuck over one ear. The Carpeted Man took a few steps and fell victim to the heat again, dropping onto the pavement.

Arthur helped the Tick into the back of a waiting ambulance. "Don't worry, Tick," he said. "We're going to the hospital."

El Seed wandered through his greenhouse, his petals drooping. "Oh, busy Bee Twins," he said to his helpers, "what's the use?"

The Bee Twins tried to cheer him up. "Come on, El Seed. Don't feel so down. You're good at this. We love you."

El Seed sprayed a potted plant. "But I spilled all the vitalizer on that big blue monkey."

"We're making more," the Bee Twins said. "Lots more."

El Seed looked at his watch. "There's no time. I have to return the airplane to the rental place by tomorrow morning. I heard they start charging by the hour if you're late."

"You can fly at dawn," the Bee Twins suggested. "Besides, the revolution has already begun."

El Seed shook his head. "A few uppity trees in the park is no revolution! I wanted a moment. There was no moment."

The Bee Twins gestured toward all the flowers in the greenhouse. "They look up to you."

El Seed started to smile. "You know, you're right. I shouldn't be so hard on myself. After all, I am El Seed!" He struck a heroic pose. "I am the self-proclaimed liberator of the plant population!" He turned to his assistants. "I realize my mistake now! The City is no place to start a plant revolution. We have an army right here!" He walked to the door and looked outside at the sweeping rows of corn that surrounded the farm. "It's all around us. And it's enormous!"

Meanwhile, at the City Hospital, the Tick was telling Arthur, "I'm feeling much better now." The Tick's head was surrounded by dandelion petals. He was thinking clearly again and he was no longer glowing green.

Arthur said, "You've got to see a doctor about this."

Now the Tick's head was covered with soft white dandelion seeds. "No, really," the Tick said. "I feel full of life!" Arthur sneezed and blew the soft white fuzz off the Tick's head.

A doctor came and examined the Tick. The doctor poked and prodded and puzzled. "Well," he said, "I've never seen anything like it. This calls for expensive testing!" He took the Tick down the hall to another room. They strapped him to a table and slid him into a special scanning machine. A pumpkin patch was sprouting on the Tick's chest. The doctor stared at the computer screen with alarm. He turned to Arthur. "Your friend has got pits!"

In the hospital waiting room down the hall, other heroes were coming in for treatment. The plant riot had taken its toll. Many heroes had suffered minor injuries and severe splinters. The Civic-minded Five were there. Captain Mucilage had one arm in a sling. Sitting next to him, the Carpeted Man was trying to catch his breath. His face was red and he was sweating.

Captain Mucilage said to him, "If you'd just take off that stupid suit you wouldn't keep getting overheated."

"But I'm the Carpeted Man! Without the suit, I am nothing!"

The Four-legged Man sat with his head bandaged, listening to the City's mysterious dark avenger, Die Fledermaus, who had his arm in a sling.

"I didn't even want to be involved!" Die Fledermaus complained. "I got jumped by a hedge! Where are the cops in this town?" He turned and saw a small fern sitting placidly on the table next to him. He jerked back in fear.

The Tick was covered in broccoli. "I hate broccoli! And yet, in a certain sense, I am broccoli."

The doctor said, "Tick, I have the results of your tests."

"Lay it on me, Doc."

"Let me be honest." The doctor looked at his clipboard. "I don't know anything about this condition. But, offhand, I'd say you've got twelve hours."

Arthur was shocked. "Twelve hours? And then what?"

"Well," said the doctor, "he may end up . . . a vegetable!"

The Tick said, "Man!" and sprouted green peppers.

4

Oh, Yeah? You and What Army of Corn?

Arthur asked, "What do we do now?"

The Tick plucked a pepper off himself and said, "We find the vegetable villain who did this to me and get the antidote!"

"There's an antidote?"

"Villains always have antidotes," the Tick said. "They're funny that way."

Arthur nodded and said, "Okay. There's an antidote and the flowerhead guy's got it. So where is he?" The Tick thought about the question as Arthur continued, "He could be anywhere. But he rented that crop duster, right?" The Tick thought about that question as Arthur continued, "And there's only one place I know where you can rent a crop duster!"

The bus stopped to let the Tick and Arthur off at Jeff's Pay 'n' Spray—All-Night Crop Duster Rental. It was already late at night. It had been a long bus ride to the farmland outside the City. The Tick was sprouting lettuce. Arthur pressed the intercom button on the airplane hangar.

"Hello," came a voice, "this is Jeff."

Arthur said, "Hi, Jeff. Listen, did you rent a crop duster to a guy with a flower for a head?"

Jeff answered, "Hey, I rent to a lot of people. What kind of flower? I'm very busy!"

The Tick pressed the intercom button and pressed his mouth against the speaker. He said loudly, "Jeff? This is the Tick. Where can we find this guy? It's a medical emergency."

Jeff said, "All right. I rented a plane to El Seed this morning. He's staying at the old abandoned greenhouse. But it's a ways down the road."

The Tick and Arthur headed down the country road at a run. After several hours, they slowed to a trot. After several more hours, they were walking. Then they spotted the headlights of a vehicle coming up the road, going their way.

"Oh, thank heavens!" Arthur said. "A car's coming. Tick, flag it down!"

The Tick raised his arms and waved at the oncoming vehicle, causing several bunches of bananas that were growing on him to sway. "Stop! Medical emergency!"

A truck roared past them. As the red taillights vanished up the road they faintly heard a delighted chorus of "Yeeees!"

"Were those *trees*?" asked Arthur. The Tick and Arthur kept walking.

As the sun rose, El Seed leapt into his crop duster. He pulled on his goggles while the Bee Twins cranked up the engine. El Seed taxied down the dirt road and took off, ready to spray his army to attention!

The Tick and Arthur were very tired when the sun rose. The lilies that grew on the Tick were drooping. Arthur looked at his watch and said, "We've only got an hour left."

"Then it will be my finest hour," the Tick said. He looked at the cornfields on the side of the road. "How far did Jeff say it was to El Seed's?"

Arthur answered, "He said it was a ways."

"Well, how many blocks is that?" The Tick suddenly heard the familiar sound of an airplane. He turned to see the crop duster barreling down on them. He and Arthur ran into the cornfield as the plane swooped over them. They fell to the ground and covered their heads as the duster released a fine green mist into the field. Suddenly the corn began to rustle and pull up its roots. Arthur glanced up. He and the Tick were surrounded by corn, each plant staring down at them with its corncob menacingly raised.

El Seed laughed an evil laugh as he flew back to the greenhouse. "So long, monkeys! No one could survive that much corn!"

When the Tick and Arthur stood up, they saw that they were surrounded by thousands and thousands of corn soldiers. Arthur asked, "Tick, can you do corn?"

The Tick thought for a second. "I don't know. I've

never tried." He clenched his muscles, including his brain, and concentrated on corn, nothing but corn. And suddenly, ears of corn sprouted all over his body. The corn soldiers stopped in their tracks and looked at him.

"Hi, guys!" the Tick called out to them.

The corn soldiers ignored the Tick, thinking he was one of them, and grabbed Arthur. The Tick stopped them.

"It's okay, boys. He's with me." The corn looked at him again. Then they released Arthur.

The corn soliders started marching toward the greenhouse. The Tick and Arthur fell into step, trying to blend in with the crowd. El Seed was waiting for his army on the greenhouse balcony. He spoke into a microphone, "Soldiers of Corn, lend me your ears!"

The Tick leaned over to Arthur with a pained expression. "Oooh, that's bad."

El Seed laughed. "Heh, heh. Already I joke and I don't even rule the world yet. You are the glorious army of El Seed! That's me! I am on a big power trip and you're coming with me!" The Bee Twins flew among the corn, passing out pens and clipboards. "My lovely assistants will pass out medical waiver forms and ballpoint pens. Please print clearly!"

"He's a madman!" the Tick said.

The Bee Twins heard him and buzzed up to the heroes. "What kind of corn soldiers are you?"

"We're colonels," the Tick and Arthur answered. And before the Bee Twins could expose them, the Tick and Arthur knocked them out. Arthur looked at his watch. "The twelve hours is almost up. We've got to get the antidote!"

The two heroes sneaked through the corn as El Seed began to ramble. "When I was at the agricultural college, I learned three things. One, never stand behind a cow. Two, people and plants can never live in harmony." The Tick and Arthur got into the greenhouse through a side door and made their way up behind El Seed, who was saying, "Three, if you really want something, you take it!" The Tick's great blue arm reached out and yanked El Seed back into the greenhouse.

"Okay, El Seed!" the Tick said. "Where's the antidote?"

El Seed grinned. "What antidote?"

Arthur shouted, "Thirty seconds!"

The Tick said, "Listen, I don't have time for any of this villain banter!" He shook El Seed hard enough to loosen several petals from his head.

"Oh," El Seed said woozily. "That antidote. It's right over there." He pointed to a spray bottle of red liquid labeled ANTIDOTE that sat on a nearby shelf.

The Tick grabbed the bottle and sprayed himself red.

Meanwhile, outside the greenhouse, the beige sedan of the Civic-minded Five pulled to a stop. The doors opened and the familiar cry of "Let's make a difference!" rang out. But before any hero could leap out of the car, they were surrounded by an unruly mob of corn. The doors slammed shut.

"Let's get out of here!" Captain Mucilage yelled. The corn soliders began to rock the car. "Roll up the windows!" The Carpeted Man turned to Jungle Janet and asked, "Is it warm in here or is it me?"

* * *

Back inside the greenhouse, the Tick was no longer sprouting. He was cured. So Arthur suggested, "We can use the crop duster to spray that antidote on the corn army!"

The Tick liked the idea. "Ooh! Plane ride!"

As they raced for the airplane, El Seed stumbled back onto the balcony. He grabbed the microphone. "Hello? Corn army?" He pointed at the Tick and Arthur running for the crop duster. "Destroy them!"

The Tick climbed into the cockpit while Arthur cranked the propeller. The corn army closed in on them. The plane lurched forward as Arthur climbed in. They took off, scattering corn plants, and released a fine red mist over the entire area.

El Seed screamed, "Noooo! I hate this!"

In the airplane, Arthur leaned forward. He had to yell over the noise of the wind and the motor. "This is fantastic! I love being a superhero!"

The Tick smiled. "I knew you would!"

The corn army returned to being normal crops. They sank their roots back into the ground and stopped moving. Of course, they weren't in straight, orderly rows like before.

The Civic-minded Five got out of their car and nabbed El Seed and the Bee Twins. The Four-legged man said to El Seed, "All right, sir. You've had your fun. We're putting you under citizens' arrest." Feral Boy started chewing on an ear of corn. Four-legged Man yelled at him. "Feral Boy! Don't put that in your mouth! It was moving two minutes ago!"

Back in the airplane, the Tick was saying, "You know, when a tomato grows out of your forehead, it gets you thinking. What do we know about anything? Life is just a big, wild, crazy tossed salad. But you don't eat it! You live it!" He flew toward the rising sun. "Isn't it great!"

On a highway far away, a green pickup truck roared past a sign that read LAS VEGAS CITY LIMITS. The trees in the truck yelled "Yeeeee!" in delight.

Part 6

THE TICK
VS.
MR. MENTAL

1

The Tick Loses His Mind

The waterfront district of the City was a seamy and dangerous part of town. It was always dark and misty. It was home to criminals and villains. It was not the sort of place where you would usually find the Tick and Arthur unless they were patrolling for criminals. But tonight the heroic duo were sitting in the Evil Eye Café. Their table was next to the stage and they were drinking fruit juice from juice boxes with little umbrellas stuck in them. The Tick was enjoying the musical stylings of blues accordionist Lotta Velour. Arthur was studying the invitation that they had received, asking them to come to the Evil Eye Café for a free "Night to Remember."

When Lotta Velour finished her song, the Tick applauded wildly and said, "Ah! What a show! What atmosphere! What fun! And for free!"

"I don't know about this place," Arthur said. Many of the customers in the café looked like the criminal vermin that had attended Chairface Chippendale's birthday party several weeks before. A large, hulking man covered with tattoos sat at the next table. There was a dagger stuck in his table. "It doesn't seem wholesome." Arthur looked at the invitation again. "And who'd want to treat us to it?"

The Tick said, "Obviously it's some citizen that we've helped, expressing his or her gratitude. Come on, Arthur. Live a little!" He lifted his juice box. "The night is young and we have umbrellas in our drinks! What could go wrong in a swell place like the Evil Eye?"

The Tick could not see the sinister red eye staring out at him through the curtain. The eye belonged to Mr. Mental, who was backstage laughing. He was a small, bald man who wore a long black cape with a high collar and a costume with the word *Mental* on the chest.

"They're here!" he cried. "I *told* you the invitation would work! Soon the Tick will be my slave!"

Minda, Mr. Mental's assistant, was standing next to him peering through the curtains. Her name, as she would tell everyone who mispronounced it, was pronounced "Mine-da." She wore a pink leotard covered with sparkles and feathers. She also wore a crown set with jewels and feathers, and a long feathery boa. "You didn't tell me he was so big."

Mr. Mental said, "Ah, but his brain is the size of a cherry pit and it's mine for the taking."

"Good heavens!" the Tick cried with shock. He opened and closed his little drink umbrella. "It works!"

Onstage, Lotta Velour said, "And now, the Evil Eye is proud to present the world's greatest mentalist—the amazing Mr. Mental!"

Mr. Mental and Minda came out onstage with a flourish. The Tick clapped loudly while Arthur politely applauded. "Thank you, Lotta."

The Tick leaned toward Arthur. "I love a good mentalist!"

"Good evening, ladies and gentlemen," Mr. Mental addressed the audience. "Welcome." He placed a blindfold over his eyes. "I will begin by donning this blindfold while my beautiful assistant, Minda, enters the audience." Minda stopped at the table of the tattooed hulking man and whispered in his ear. He grinned and handed her something. "Now," Mr. Mental continued, "I will demonstrate my amazing mind by identifying objects selected at random by the beautiful Minda." He touched his forehead in concentration. "I'm seeing . . . is it . . . a hangman's noose?"

Minda held up the object that the hulking man had given her. It was indeed a hangman's noose. "Yes, Mr. Mental!" she acknowledged. The audience gasped in amazement.

The Tick leaned over to Arthur again. "Telepathy, Arthur! Incredible!"

"And now, Minda," Mr. Mental instructed, "another object, please!" He pressed his fingers to his forehead, concentrating his amazing powers. "Ah, I'm seeing a *group* of objects. This is a hard one!" He strained. "Are they . . . a timing clock, a fuse wire, and a package of high explosives?"

Minda held up her hand for the crowd to see. She was indeed holding all the objects that Mr. Mental had just described! The crowd gasped in amazement again. And they burst into applause and cheers.

Mr. Mental removed his blindfold and said, "For my next phenomenal feat, I will require a volunteer from the audience." He pointed at the Tick. "You, sir!" The Tick stood up nervously. "Give him a hand, everybody!" The Tick went up onstage next to short Mr. Mental.

Mr. Mental looked up at the hero and chuckled. "My, my, aren't you a big fellow." Then he turned to the audience. "And now, a demonstration of the marvelous and always-amusing powers of hypnosis." He looked at the Tick. "Tell me, what is your greatest fear? Your worst nightmare?"

"That's easy," the Tick answered. "Being cooped up in an office all day. Phones ringing! Keyboards clacking! No superheroing!"

Mr. Mental reared back and used his special finger-wiggling hypnotizer hand gesture and his eyeballs turned into red spirals. The Tick stared at him. "Tick," Mr. Mental said in his special hypnotizer voice, "your mind is under my control. Your will is now mine!"

The Tick's eyes turned into red spirals. "Whoa. Okay, my will is yours."

"You work in an office," Mr. Mental said to the Tick. The Tick looked terrified and beads of sweat appeared on his face. He began to move his hands as if he were typing. Mr. Mental continued, "And you really love it, don't you?" The Tick's expression changed. He relaxed and smiled, nodding and waving to unseen co-workers as he continued to type. "Now," Mr. Mental said, "cluck like a chicken." The Tick clucked like a chicken. "Now, dance like a ballerina." The Tick began a series of fantastic ballet movements, spinning, leaping, and turning with superb

grace. He did a magnificent scissors kick and landed. The audience applauded.

"Thank you. Thank you." Mr. Mental did his hypnotizer hand gesture again. The Tick's eyes returned to normal. Mr. Mental ushered him off the stage. "Hasn't he been a great sport, folks?"

The Tick sat down next to Arthur, who said, "Tick? Are you all right?"

"I guess so."

"Well, I think we've sampled enough atmosphere for one night. Let's go home."

Later that night, Mr. Mental and Minda stood on an old pier at the riverfront. "There it is," Mr. Mental said, pointing to a small, rocky island in the river. On the island was a concrete-and-steel blockhouse surrounded by a high fence and barbed wire. Spotlights lit up the island. "The Pendecker laboratory."

Minda asked, "That gizmo you want is in there?"

"It's no mere gizmo, my dear." Mr. Mental looked through binoculars at the island. He could see a sign on the building that read PENDECKER ADVANCED RESEARCH DIVISION: INBOARD MOTORS—OUTBOARD MOTORS. MENTAL POWERS ACCESSORIES. "It is a device that will make my mind the most powerful on Earth! Nothing will stop me!"

Minda snickered. "Yeah, right. You don't even swim. And those walls can withstand a dynamite blast."

Mr. Mental said with an evil grin, "Why do you think I forged my mind-link with the Tick?"

2

The Tick—Zombie Slave
of Evil

The Tick was having a restless night. Although he was usually quite comfortable on the sofa bed in Arthur's apartment, this night he tossed and turned. Then he heard Mr. Mental's voice in his head. "Tick!" it called.

"What?" the Tick answered. He sat up in bed. His eyes were red spirals.

"Do me a favor," Mr. Mental said. "Go to the Pendecker laboratory and bring me the box labeled THINKING CAP." The Tick rose from the sofa bed. "Oh, and Tick? Destroy anything that stands in your way!"

The Tick smashed through the front door and left the apartment. Arthur ran out to see what the noise was. "Tick?" he called. He followed the Tick's heavy footsteps up the stairs and onto the roof. "Tick? What's wrong? Where are you going?" The Tick ignored him. Arthur ran around in front of the Tick. "Stop! Tick! Wait a minute!"

The Tick swatted Arthur with his mighty arm. Arthur

fell backward and then toppled off the roof. He screamed in panic before remembering that he could fly. He pressed the button on his chest that opened his moth wings. He flew up and started following the Tick, who was leaping from rooftop to rooftop. The hypnotized hero was getting directions in his head from Mr. Mental. "Tick, hang a left on Main. Okay, now you want to go down Main for two lights."

At that time, Mr. Mental was sitting in a chair in a cheap motel trying to maintain his control over the Tick. It was hard, because Minda was sitting on the bed watching *The Mummy Speaks* on the late show. "Minda!" he shouted at her. "Would you turn that thing down? I'm controlling a mind here!"

"Control yourself," Minda said. "I'm trying to watch this."

Mr. Mental held up his hand, his thumb and forefinger an inch apart. "I'm this close to ruling the world."

Minda held up her fist. "Rule this."

Meanwhile, Arthur swooped in on the Tick, who had stopped moving. The Tick stared at him for a second, then blinked and said, "Oh. Arthur. Hi. I just had the craziest dream." Arthur tried to catch his breath. The Tick said, "Mr. Mental—the nightclub guy—he was giving me directions. I was powerless to resist."

"What kind of directions?" Arthur asked.

"I'm not sure. Something about going for a swim."

Back in the motel, Minda turned down the television so Mr. Mental could concentrate. The evil mentalist thought, "Tick! I'm still in control here." And across town, the Tick's eyes became red circles again. He mindlessly shoved Arthur and walked away.

Arthur shouted, "Try to fight it, Tick! I'll get help!"

In a diner not far away, Die Fledermaus, Crusading Chameleon, and Sewer Urchin were bored.

"So what are we going to do?" Crusading Chameleon asked.

Sewer Urchin brightened up. "You guys want to see my new place?"

Die Fledermaus looked down at him. "In the sewer? I don't think so."

Suddenly Arthur raced in. "Hey, guys! I need your help! The Tick is in trouble!"

The Tick walked like a zombie to the waterfront. He trudged straight into the river. "Euww! Slimy!" he said. But he kept walking and disappeared under the surface. Then he walked along the bottom of the river. He could hold his breath for a long time because of his immensely powerful lungs. He passed through heavy seaweed.

Covered in a thick coat of seaweed, he walked up onto the rocky island in the river. His antennae remained free. He tore through the electric fence and went straight to the concrete-and-steel blockhouse. With his amazing strength he smashed open the steel door. An alarm sounded, but the Tick did not hear it. Inside the vault he saw a steel crate marked THINKING CAP. Standing next to it was a large, powerfully built robot.

The robot fired two searing heat rays out of its eyes.

They hit the Tick in the chest but didn't stop him. The Tick advanced. When he was close enough, the robot grabbed him with its arms, which were designed to crush tanks. The Tick managed to grab the robot's head. He strained with all his might and tore it off. As the robot toppled to the ground, the Tick picked up the crate and headed back to the river.

Meanwhile, back at the pier, Arthur had arrived with the other superheroes. He was flying. "No sign of him from the air. Anything on land?"

Die Fledermaus was posing dramatically. "No. When you said he was going swimming, I knew he had to come to the river. But I see nothing. Maybe he went home and went to bed."

Sewer Urchin surfaced in the water. "I didn't find the Tick." Then he heard something behind him. A huge figure covered in seaweed broke the surface of the river right behind Sewer Urchin. All the heroes screamed at the sight of this horrible seaweed-covered swamp monster. Sewer Urchin ran for his life out of the water.

The seaweed slipped off the monster as it stomped onto the shore, revealing the Tick. Die Fledermaus pointed. "Hey! It's the Tick!" Sewer Urchin stopped running and stood there as the Tick approached. "Boy, am I glad it's you. We thought you were something dangerous." The Tick smacked Sewer Urchin to one side. Sewer Urchin crashed into the wooden pier and the spines on his costume stuck in the wood. He hung there, helpless.

Crusading Chameleon shouted, "I'll stop him!" He leapt onto the crate that the Tick carried, sticking to it with his suction-cup hands and feet. The Tick reached up

and pulled Chameleon until the rubbery suckers popped off the box. Then the Tick threw the lizard hero over next to Sewer Urchin.

Arthur and Die Fledermaus watched this fight with alarm. Arthur said, "I told you! The Tick's mind is being controlled by an evil force!"

"Oh, yes, I see." Die Fledermaus checked his watch. "Well, tell me how it all turns out." He darted away and Arthur listened to his footsteps receding into the distance.

Arthur flew up and landed in front of the plodding Tick. "You've got to fight it! Don't give in!"

Mr. Mental's voice rang in the Tick's head. "Tick! Let nothing stand in your way!"

The Tick towered over Arthur. The little sidekick stumbled back. For the first time, he was afraid of his big blue friend.

"Destroy him!" Mr. Mental commanded.

The Tick lifted the heavy metal box over his head. He was going to use it to smash Arthur!

3

The 9 to 5 Nightmare

Arthur looked up at the metal box. "Tick! Don't do this! It's Arthur! Your sidekick!"

The Tick looked confused. "Side . . . kick . . ." Then his eyes stopped spinning red. "Arthur? What's going on? What am I doing?"

"Good question," Arthur said, both frightened and annoyed.

Mr. Mental tried to regain control of the Tick's head. "Destroy him! Him and all that stands in your way. Bring me the Thinking Cap!"

The Tick shook his head, trying to think. "I don't wanna."

"Aw, c'mon," Mr. Mental said. "You gotta!"·

The Tick yelled, "Nooo!" and ran off down the street. Arthur watched, shaken and disturbed. Crusading Chameleon staggered up to him. Arthur grabbed the color-changing crusader. "Come on. Help me get Sewer Urchin down! We've got to save the Tick!"

Mr. Mental was worried. He was losing control of the Tick. Minda was reading a magazine. Mr. Mental said, "I'm losing him. I must pummel his mind, beat his will into submission! I know! I'll open the floodgates of his own worst nightmare!"

"Whatever," said Minda, not looking up.

The sky was stormy as the Tick leapt from rooftop to rooftop. He couldn't think straight. Although that usually didn't bother him, this time he knew Mr. Mental was causing it, and it really upset him. As he stopped on the edge of a roof, an office building across the street seemed to rise up and loom over him. It stretched toward him, the side of the building tearing open to become a mouth with the steel girders turning into teeth. The office building swallowed the Tick whole!

Suddenly the Tick was sitting at a desk in an office. He was typing. Computers hummed. Elevators buzzed. Keyboards clacked. The phone rang. He answered it.

He heard the computerized voice on the phone say, "You have reached the offices of the Tick's nightmare. The Tick is out of his mind right now. If you would like to leave a message, please wait for the tone. If you'd like to speak to an operator . . ."

The Tick was very frightened. "A day job?" he thought. "In an office! Noooo!"

Five of his co-workers crowded around his desk, shoving pieces of paper at him and talking at once. "Tick, here's the Shackley memo. I need this typed up in triplicate." "Henderson gave himself the promotion." "Tick! Don't forget our racquetball game, I'm going to destroy you on the court." "You're not so special. Anyone can touch-type." "Tick!" "Tick!" "Tick!"

All the noise and office chatter was drowned out by Mr. Mental's voice. "Now. No more fooling around."

The Tick was grateful that the office was gone. "No more fooling around," he agreed. The Tick was fully hypnotized again. He hurried off to Tabasco Joe's Live Bait and Lodging, where Mr. Mental and Minda were waiting.

"I've got to get some sleep," Minda said, yawning as they stood outside their room. "We've got a matinee tomorrow."

Mr. Mental shouted, raising his fist in the air. "No! Tomorrow we rule the world!"

"Yeah, right." Minda rolled her eyes.

The Tick ran up and dropped the steel crate at Mr. Mental's feet. The evil mentalist unhooked the lid and opened it. He picked up a large bowl-shaped helmet with what looked like a lawn mower engine built onto the side. The engine had a pull-cord and a choke switch.

"The Thinking Cap," Mr. Mental said with awe. He placed it on his head. "It would give an ordinary human mental abilities to rival mine. So it will give me the powers of the gods!" He yanked the pull-cord. It sputtered. He pulled again and it roared to life. The vibration of the engine caused Mr. Mental's voice to tremble. "Oooh . . . that feels nice."

"You've served your purpose, numbskull," he said to the emotionless Tick. Then the helmet developed a blue glow. Twin beams of blue energy shot from Mr. Mental's eyes, slamming into the Tick and knocking him across the street. The Tick crashed into a brick wall and it crumbled on top of him. Mr. Mental levitated off the ground, giggling like a child. Then he heard a voice yell, "Hey!"

He turned to see Arthur, Crusading Chameleon, and Sewer Urchin marching up the street toward him. Arthur shouted, "What did you do with the Tick?"

Mr. Mental floated toward the heroes. "Nothing compared to what I'm going to do to you!"

4

A Mind Is a Terrible Thing

Mr. Mental closed in on the three heroes, floating effort-lessly toward them. He lifted his arm and blue beams shot out, lifting them all into the air. He began to juggle them. Then he threw them where he'd thrown the Tick, into the pile of bricks that had once been a wall.

Mr. Mental continued down the street. Using the power of his mind, he flipped cars over and twisted street-lights into pretzel shapes. He laughed like a madman. He was unstoppable.

The Tick sat up in the brick pile. He groaned. He looked around and saw Arthur, Crusading Chameleon, and Sewer Urchin. "Hey, guys," he said.

Arthur struggled to his feet. "Tick! Mr. Mental's going to take over the world with that Thinking Cap!"

The Tick looked off down the street. "That rat!" He helped the other heroes stand up. "Let's get him, boys!"

Arthur said, "Wait. He's too powerful with that

Thinking Cap. But it runs on an internal combustion engine."

Sewer Urchin asked, "So? What's your point?"

Arthur began, "The internal combustion engine—perfected by Nikolau August Otto in the last half of the nineteenth century—runs on a carefully controlled mixture of gasoline and air." Sewer Urchin and Crusading Chameleon looked at each other and rolled their eyes. The Tick listened carefully. Arthur continued: "The mixture is fed into a cylinder and ignited by a spark plug. This causes a small explosion, which drives the piston, creating the movement of the engine." The Tick struggled to grasp the information. "The choke valve controls how much air enters the fuel mixture. Without air, the fuel cannot ignite and floods the engine, causing it to stall."

"So?" the Tick asked.

Arthur struck the palm of his hand with his fist. "We've got to get close enough to that helmet to pull the choke—and *flood his mind*!"

The sun was rising. Mr. Mental continued his reign of terror. He shot blue beams out everywhere, cracking the street and breaking windows. He glided near a small park, where there was a fountain with a stone column in the middle of it. As he floated over a manhole, the cover slid back and Sewer Urchin jumped out. He grabbed Mr. Mental's feet.

Mr. Mental looked down. "Don't mess with me, you fool! I'm cooking with gas!"

Mr. Mental didn't see Crusading Chameleon on a nearby billboard. The hero had blended his colors to the blue-and-white advertisement for Honesty Cola. As Mr. Mental tried to shake Sewer Urchin off his feet, Crusading Chameleon leapt onto the villain, seizing him around the waist.

At the same time, Arthur flew overhead and went into a power dive. As he neared Mr. Mental's head, he reached for the helmet.

Suddenly, Mr. Mental used a massive burst of energy to knock the three heroes off him. Then he gathered them up in a big blue force bubble. He used another stream of energy to rip the stone column from its place in the middle of the fountain. Using his mind, he swung the column at the blue force bubble like a baseball bat. "Batter up, boys!"

Just then the Tick leapt off a roof and landed on top of Mr. Mental with a great thud. This caused Mr. Mental to drop the three other heroes and the stone column. The Tick and Mr. Mental were spinning in the air. The Tick clutched the Thinking Cap with all of his awesomely spectacular strength to keep from being thrown off.

The Tick struggled against the tremendous energy pouring from Mr. Mental's eyes. He strained, reaching for the choke on the helmet. Using all his might, he grabbed it and pulled it out.

The engine on the helmet sputtered and coughed. "Noooo!" screamed Mr. Mental. Then the engine stalled and died. Mr. Mental and the Tick dropped to the ground with a big splat. The helmet fell off Mr. Mental's head. The Tick grabbed the villain and lifted him off the ground.

Mr. Mental groaned, "Oh, the headache I've got."

The Tick said, "I'd say you deserve it! You're a bad act, Mr. Mental!"

That night at the local diner, the Tick and Arthur gathered with Crusading Chameleon and Sewer Urchin. They sat on the stools at the counter and drank coffee. Arthur drank decaffeinated. Crusading Chameleon liked cappuccino. Sewer Urchin enjoyed a blend of coffees from Sumatra and Tanzania, robust but not too bitter. The Tick liked any coffee if it had sugar in it. Lots of sugar.

As the Tick poured more sugar into his cup, he said, "The human mind is a dangerous plaything, boys. When it's used for evil, watch out!" He stirred his coffee with great fervor. Coffee sloshed out of his cup onto the counter. "But when it's used for good . . . things are much nicer! And let's try to keep that in mind!"

They all nodded in agreement and sipped.

COMING SOON !
MORE ADVENTURES OF

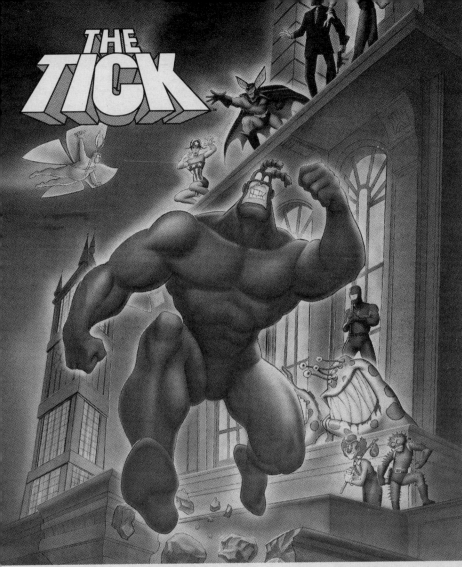

THE TICK

COMING TO SEGA™ GENESIS AND SUPER NES® NOVEMBER 1994